IF LIFE WERE FAIR

Sharon L. Tocchini

ISBN: 978-1-64669-987-2   (Paperback Edition)
ISBN: 978-1-64669-988-9   (Hardcover Edition)
ISBN: 978-1-64669-986-5   (E-book Edition)

Some characters and events in this book are fictitious. Any similarity to real persons, living or dead, is coincidental and not intended by the author.

Book Ordering Information

Phone Number: 347-901-4929 or 347-901-4920
Email: info@globalsummithouse.com
Global Summit House
www.globalsummithouse.com

Printed in the United States of America

DEDICATION

With love to my siblings.

Without you, the journey would have been meaningless.

ACKNOWLEDGMENTS

The writer never writes alone. A writer never puts pen to paper or fingertips to computer keys without the tremendous ongoing help from others. Those who assist the writer in any way write the story as well. Thank you to those who assisted in being part of the making of this story.

A specific thank you to retired homicide detective Steven L. Antuna, who was the inspiration for the detective in this story. Thank you for sharing your job experiences and expertise and being so very generous in your continuing critique as the story took shape.

To those who were generous enough to give of their time and knowledge, which ultimately helped sharp scenes and effected details of the story that would not have been available otherwise. Thank you.

Mark R. Olin, deputy director, crime laboratory
Robert L. Stratton, unit technical lead /
forensic scientist supervisor, crime lab
Theresa Willis, deputy sheriff, Van Cise-Simonet Detention Center
Dhon, O. H., officer of Denver Police Department

Thank you to my fellow writers who have gone before, who have published books to teach, assist, and help the novice writer. To the teachers of the art who have generously shared their knowledge and stories of past efforts. Thank you to all those people who give of themselves for the betterment of others.

* * *

CHAPTER
ONE

The phone rang twice. A stoic voice answered, "Nine-one-one. Where's your emergency?"

"Four-two-five Dudley Court, Pleasantville." The voice crackled with fear.

"What's the nature of your emergency?"

"My mother's lying on the floor, facedown. I—I don't know if she's alive or not. She's bleeding from her head."

"Do you see or hear her breathing?'

"No. She's not moving. I don't want to touch her," the stress and fear were evident in the caller's voice.

"Okay, stay where you are, we'll send the paramedics right away."

"Okay."

"Stay on the line with me."

"Okay."

Helen could hear the sirens in the distance with the sound getting closer with every second that passed. She walked closer to the motionless body with the cell phone still held against her ear, and bent closer to examine the portion of her mother's head that was covered with blood when she noticed the sirens had grown louder, as if they were out in front of the house. She jumped slightly when someone knocked hard on the door.

"I think they're here," she informed the 911 operator.

"Okay, I'll let them take it from here," said the calm voice.

"Paramedics," the masculine voice announced loudly from the doorway.

Helen walked toward the front door and swung open the glass storm door to allow a tall, husky dark-haired male in, followed by a small blond female, both were dressed in dark-blue shirts and slacks. She noticed a bright-yellow patch with a medical insignia centered at the top of the sleeve.

"I'm Brad. This is Samantha. Where is your mother," he said hurriedly.

Helen pointed toward the kitchen, "Over there."

Brad and Samantha set their equipment down next to the motionless female. Brad knelt down next to the body, reached toward the elderly woman's neck, placed the tips of his index and middle finger on the carotid artery, and concentrated quietly for the next sixty seconds. "No pulse, and the body is cold to the touch," he said as he glanced up at Samantha and then looked up at Helen. "I'm sorry to inform you, but there's no pulse. Your mother is probably dead."

Tears began to fall down Helen's face. "I was afraid of that," she said.

Samantha rose and walked toward Helen. "If you wouldn't mind stepping over here to the other room so I can get some information from you. Brad will take care of your mother." She put her hand on Helen's upper arm and gently nudged her toward the living area near the front door and allowed Helen to take a seat while she removed a small spiral-bound notebook and pen from her shirt pocket. Samantha pulled a small ottoman as close to Helen as possible, in case she might need assistance.

"I understand that you're the daughter, is that right?"

"Yes."

"What is your full name?" Samantha poised her pen for writing.

"Helen St. Claire."

"Where do you live?"

"I live just five blocks from here." She paused. "Oh, you want the address, 618 Caverns Drive."

"Thank you."

They both hesitated and turned toward the front door when they heard it unlatch. A young uniformed policeman walked in, waved in greeting, and continued toward Brad, who stood near the kitchen.

"What do we have here?" he asked Brad as he looked over the body without touching it.

"It looks like trauma to the head. No pulse and cold to the touch when we arrived. That's her daughter talking to Sam. I've called Dr. Tenzel to inform him there are no vital signs, and he's pronounced her."

The officer spoke into the small square black microphone attached to the epaulet on his left shoulder. "Dispatch, we have a suspicious death. Can you send my supervisor and some backup to the 425 Dudley Court address?"

Dispatch acknowledged. "We'll send homicide out there."

"Ten-four."

The officer walked over to Helen and Sam to listen to the questions Sam was asking.

Sam turned and looked at the short, thin officer with black hair and noticed sunglasses hanging from his shirt pocket.

"I'll let you take over," she said as she rose from her seat and handed him the piece of paper she had been taking notes on.

He glanced at the notes Sam had made. "No meds, no current doctor's care, no illnesses other than acute Alzheimer's disease, rents home, five children, Helen the oldest, spouse deceased three-plus years ago. Great, thanks," he said as Samantha went to gather her equipment. Then she followed Brad to the front door.

Brad opened the storm door, allowing Sam to pass through first as he turned to speak to the officer. "We'll write up a statement before we leave."

"Great." The officer turned toward Helen and reached out his hand in greeting. "I'm Officer Jeffrey Osmond. I've called for a detective, since the cause of death isn't clear. I'm sorry for your loss, but I have to ask you a few more questions. Is that okay?"

"Yes."

"Have you noticed anything unusual?"

"No."

"Have you noticed any forced entry?"

"No. The front door was locked when I arrived, and I haven't looked around."

"Did your mother live here alone?"

"Yes."

"Should there be anyone else in the house right now?"

"No."

"I need you to step outside on the front porch until another officer arrives. I'm going to take a look around."

He led Helen through the opened door then turned while pulling his Sig P229. He held it at his side as he proceeded toward the north side of the home, which comprised the bedrooms. He could feel the warmth of adrenaline rise within his body as he instinctively anticipated confronting an unfamiliar individual somewhere in the house. He had learned during his three years on the force that this was actually a healthy source of fear. He had been taught that it was enough fear to make a person cautious and alert but not too much fear such that a person became paralyzed and prevented them from acting as necessary to protect themselves.

He quietly walked to the bedroom to his left, which was the master bedroom, and peered around the corner. Nothing out of the ordinary was apparent. The bed was unmade, and a pile of crumpled clothes lay in the far corner. He approached the closet and slowly slid the sliding door open, cocked his head to view the bottom of the closet looking for legs and feet that would signal an intruder, saw nothing, and then pushed the sparse clothing to one side and then the other. He saw nothing that would put him on alert. He then looked into the master bathroom through the open door. He noted that the shower curtain was pulled tightly against the wall, allowing no place to hide in the tub. Before leaving the bedroom, he knelt down next to the bed and lifted the bed skirt to make sure no one was hiding under the bed. Nothing. He rose and walked back to the hallway that had led him to the master bedroom. He poked his head into the second bathroom in the middle of the hallway, and seeing that there was nowhere to hide, he went on to the room at the end of the hall where the door to the room was shut but not latched. He pulled his pistol up closer to his chest and slowly pushed the door open with his free hand. He unconsciously sucked in a quick, short breath when he saw hundreds of eyes peering back at him.

4

He instinctively readied his weapon using both hands and then grinned and allowed the tension in his shoulders to relax when he realized the eyes belonged to what appeared to be hundreds of antique dolls, which lined the shelves of all four walls, and many more standing on the floor, all gazing at him intently. He looked carefully among the dolls as his mind conjured the closet scene from *E.T.* When he was certain there were no extraterrestrial or other uninvited intruder standing among them, he holstered his weapon and returned to Helen. He held the glass door open for her to reenter the home.

"Everything is clear. You can come in and be seated again. I still have a couple of questions for you." He sat across from her and waited for her to get comfortably seated.

"Can you tell me what happened here?"

"You mean when I got here?" Helen's voice was a bit shaky.

"Yes, ma'am."

"Well, I came over to check on my mother as I usually do on Mondays—that's my day."

"What do you mean by your day?" the officer interrupted.

"I have a brother and a younger sister that come by to see my mother during the week. I don't speak to my sister, but she comes on Fridays, and my brother comes on Wednesdays."

"You said you don't speak to your sister. Why's that?"

"We had a huge family fight because she brought in a conservator to handle my mother's affairs—it's in the courts right now."

"Does that mean it's not settled yet?"

"No, it's not. It just keeps going for some reason or another."

"Okay, so you came over to the house this morning, right? Can you please continue?"

"I unlocked the front door and called for my mom. There was no answer. When I came in, I saw her lying on the floor by the kitchen, and I called 911."

"Did you touch her at all?"

"No. I didn't know what to do, so I called 911."

The officer made notes as they talked.

"So you said the front door was locked when you got here. Are you sure the door was locked?'

"Yes."

"Did you notice anything out of the ordinary? Like signs of forced entry or anything out of place?"

"No."

"When was the last time you talked to your mother?"

"Yesterday. I called her to see how she was doing."

"And what was the outcome of that call?"

"She was fine."

"Is there anyone else who might have come by the house yesterday, last evening, or earlier today?"

Helen paused and thought for a second or two, "No, not that I know of." Helen looked over at her mother's body lying on the floor, and the tears began to well up in the corner of her eyes. She wiped them away with the tips of her fingers.

"Is there anything else you think I should know?" asked the officer.

"I'll bet my little sister did this," she said as the tears flowed more freely. Helen wrestled with her purse looking for a tissue to wipe away the tears.

"Why do you think that?" said the officer, his attention now peaked.

CHAPTER

TWO

The storm door opened, and an attractive, stocky dark-skinned gentleman dressed in what appeared to be an expensive suit and tie, with polished classic leather loafers, and with well-cut salt-and-pepper hair, came in.

Officer Osmond stood up to address the detective. "This is Helen St. Claire, the daughter of the deceased. She found the body." He turned toward Helen. "This is Detective Chavez. He'll be in charge of the investigation." He stepped back out of the way so the detective could shake hands with Helen. "He'll take it from here. I'll fill him in on the questions we've already gone over."

Helen nodded, wiped her eyes, and waited quietly.

The two policemen walked over to the body. Officer Osmond informed the detective he had checked the house and found it to be devoid of any other persons and then reviewed the questions he and Helen had covered. He lowered his voice slightly, "She made a comment that I think is important."

"What's that?" asked the detective.

"She said she thinks her little sister did this to her mother."

"Why does she think that?'

"We didn't get that far. You walked in at that point in time, and I never got an explanation."

"Thank you, Officer Osmond. I'll take over from here. There are a couple of crime scene investigators who just arrived. Would you mind taking Mrs. St. Claire out to your car, and I'll be out to talk to her when I'm done here?"

"Yes, sir." Officer Osmond handed the detective the notebook with barely legible notes on several pages.

Detective Chavez knelt down to view the bloody head then stood up to view the entire body and its surroundings. Several people came through the door and addressed the detective. "Hi, fellows. Go ahead and do your thing." He opened his pad folio made of high-quality leather to make notes as the crime scene investigators photographed and videoed the home. He poised his gold-plated mechanical pencil then waited for them to call out details that needed to be notated as he diagramed the scene for his report. He would need the measurements of all walls and structures in relation to the body in order to present the scene accurately for his report and perhaps the jury, should they find it necessary to visit the actual scene. He smiled as he heard the senior crime investigator tell the rookie to take the "dumb end" of the tape. He recalled that the rookies on any investigative team always got their own sort of hazing. He continued to write. He watched as the team dusted for prints on the kitchen counters, doorknobs, refrigerator, and numerous other areas that might prove fruitful for evidence.

Thirty minutes later, Detective Chavez walked over to Helen, who had been brought back into the house at his request, and sat down directly across from her. "I'm sorry about your mother. You've been through a lot today, but I do have to get a little more information, and I'll need you to sign a statement of what occurred. Mrs. St. Claire, would you be willing to come down to the station with me?"

"Yes, I guess."

"You seem hesitant, Mrs. St. Claire. Is there a problem with that?"

"No, it's just that my husband will be expecting me home, so I should probably call him and tell him what happened and where I'll be."

"That's a good idea. Why don't you do that? I also need to request the key to the house so I can lock up after we're done here and request that none of the family enter the premises from this point forward. By the way, have you been given the opportunity to call your family?"

"No, I haven't called anyone yet." Helen's voice was more stable now, and the tears had stopped. She handed him a key ring that held a small chrome-colored house on it, and one key.

"Why don't you take a few minutes to do that while I talk to the investigators? And then we'll head down to the station."

"Okay." She pulled her phone from her purse and began to dial.

Detective Chavez walked around the house to look for signs of forced entry that might have been missed earlier. He went out to the garage, which was off the kitchen, and noted the door that led outside was left ajar and unlocked. He pulled a handkerchief from his back-pants pocket and used it to open the door wider without disturbing any evidence that might prove useful in the investigation. He walked around the outside of the home to check for forced entry, saw nothing, and came back in ready to talk to Helen if she was done informing the relatives of their mother's death.

He addressed the crime scene investigator that stood in the kitchen. "The door to the outside was ajar. It needs to be printed before you go."

The investigator responded with a nod.

Helen was done and waiting patiently for the detective. He approached. "Mrs. St. Claire, did you notice anything missing or out of place when you first came into the house?"

"No. The door was locked when I got here, and nothing seemed out of place, until I saw my mother on the floor, but I didn't look around the house." She glanced down at her mother's hands, which were stretched out in front of her. "She doesn't have her rings on." Helen said.

"Tell me about that." Detective Chavez urged, feeling that Helen had been surprised by this new revelation.

"She always wore her rings. She loved her jewelry."

"Can you give me a description of the rings you're talking about?" Detective Chavez pulled a stylish black Montblanc pen from inside his jacket, twisted it into writing position, and waited for Helen to begin.

"Yes, one was diamond shaped with three or four rows of smaller diamonds in a white-gold setting. The other was an eternity band with eight diamonds across the top, also in a white-gold setting." There was no hesitation in the description of her mother's jewelry.

"You seem to know a lot about jewelry, Mrs. St. Claire."

"Don't all women know a lot about jewelry?" she said defensively.

"Where would your mother normally keep her jewelry?"

"In her bedroom."

"Would you mind accompanying me to her bedroom to look around?"

"No." Helen got up and headed to the hallway and turned left toward the rear of the house.

Detective Chavez followed. "It's important that you don't touch anything, Mrs. St. Claire—just look."

"Okay." Helen held her hands to her chest, one hand covering the other. She looked at the tops of the long, dark cherrywood dresser and the two smaller, matching nightstands, all of which were covered with a layer of thick dust on top of white linen dresser scarfs.

Detective Chavez watched her every move. He sensed she knew the bedroom well as she peered carefully around the knickknacks and the jewelry box that sat atop the large dresser.

Helen pointed cautiously to the rectangular wooden box, "That's her jewelry box."

The detective took his pen and carefully placed it under one corner to lift the lid. "Take a look inside, Mrs. St. Claire, and tell me if you see the rings you mentioned your mother normally wore."

Helen leaned forward and peeked in the box, making every effort not to touch anything, intentionally or unintentionally. "No, I don't see them in there."

The detective closed the lid slowly and turned to leave. "Thank you. Do you see anything out of the ordinary in this room?"

"No. Everything seems normal." Helen followed the detective out of the room and returned to the living room.

"Officer Osmond had mentioned that you think your younger sister might have something to do with the demise of your mother. Can you tell me why you think that?'

Helen's defensive tone of voice was back. "Yes, she stands to inherit the largest portion of my mother's estate. Wouldn't that make her a suspect?"

"Everyone is a suspect in a homicide, Mrs. St. Claire," he said sternly. "Are you ready to head downtown so you can help us with some more information?" He waved his hand toward the door as if to usher Helen in that direction.

CHAPTER
THREE

As the detective and Helen headed for the front door, another gentleman reached for the door and opened it from the opposite side.

Detective Chavez looked at him and then at his watch. "Running late, Dr. Charlotte?" he asked in a sarcastic tone.

The forensic pathologist was a tall, thin middle-aged man with blond hair and blue eyes. He was dressed in black slacks, light-blue shirt, and dark-blue-and-red-striped tie. "Sorry I'm late getting here, Detective Chavez."

"Helen, I need to fill the good doctor in on the circumstances. I'll have Officer Osmond take you down to the station, and I'll be down there shortly."

"Okay." Helen stood by the front door waiting for Officer Osmond to show her to his vehicle.

Detective Chavez led Dr. Charlotte over to the body lying half in the kitchen and half in the TV room. Dr. Charlotte knelt down to look over the body of the lifeless older woman.

Dr. Charlotte had been educated in Louisiana and had come to the state and county after being hired by his wife's brother, who had become county coroner the year before, so he made little or no effort to befriend his coworkers.

He examined the head wound first then rolled the body over to look for signs of rigor mortis and livor mortis in order to ascertain the time of death. He noticed that the facial muscles had begun to stiffen, a sign the body had been dead for approximately three hours. The stiffening would progress downward, in a head-to-toe direction. Rigor mortis would completely envelop the body in twelve to eighteen hours. He also noted that livor mortis had been at work as well. The elderly woman's blood had pooled in the lower portions of the body. The front of her body, which had lain against the floor, had a purplish discoloration to the skin. He pushed gently on the purplish area with the tip of his index finger. It turned white for a second before the purplish color returned. Based on his knowledge that livor mortis begins about thirty minutes after death, his review of the surroundings, and not seeing anything unusual as far as temperature or other factors that might throw his calculations off, he determined that she had probably been dead three to four hours.

Dr. Charlotte replaced the body as originally found so the crime scene investigators could resume once he had completed his initial investigation of what was, for now, being considered a crime scene, even though it was not yet clear that this incident was indeed a clear homicide situation.

A removal company would be called to take the body to the morgue, and an autopsy would be performed to determine cause of death and examine any trace evidence left on the body, at the earliest possible time.

"Any conclusions?" asked Detective Chavez as he stood and watched Dr. Charlotte during his initial inspection of the body.

"No. We'll have to do an autopsy to be sure of anything. Did you find any weapon that might have caused the blunt trauma to the head?"

"No. No murder weapon was found and no forced entry."

He stood up next to the detective. "As with any case, we won't know for sure until the autopsy is performed if this is truly a homicide."

"Yes, but evidence doesn't lie, so we'll compare notes come tomorrow." The detective walked away without waiting or wanting a reply from Dr. Charlotte. As far as he was concerned, it was better to treat a suspicious death as a crime scene rather than let evidence fall by the wayside out of ignorance, neglect, or malfeasance. He remembered being taught that the basic principle of homicide investigation was to do it right the first time, since you only got one chance at it. He walked away irritated that Dr. Charlotte wasn't following the same train of thought.

CHAPTER
FOUR

Upon arrival at the police station, Detective Chavez led Helen to a small interrogation room with off-white walls containing a table and two chairs. He directed Helen to the chair that faced the blank wall, and backed to the door they had just entered. He positioned himself in the chair across from her at the corner of the table nearest to Helen. "Can I get you something to drink, water or soda?"

"No, I'm okay, thank you."

"Mrs. St. Claire, we're here so you can provide me with more information about what occurred today concerning your mother's death and the surrounding circumstances. Again, I'm sorry about your mother's death, but we do need additional information. I'm not going to take notes or videotape our conversation. I want you to be comfortable and tell me what you can recall about the events of the day. If you can, please start at the beginning of your day, and move forward."

"Well, this morning, Bill, my husband, and I had breakfast, then I cleaned up and drove to my mother's house, unlocked the door, went in, found her lying on the floor, facedown, and called 911."

"What else did you do?"

"Just called 911."

"Are you sure? Nothing else you can remember?"

"No. That's it."

"What time was it when you arrived at your mother's home this morning?"

Helen paused, as if in thought. "Somewhere around eight."

Detective Chavez quickly became aware that Helen was not a person that would go into great detail without prodding her. He suspected he was going to have to pull every detail out of her. As he watched her, he noted that she was an ample but attractive middle-aged woman who clearly dyed her hair herself. Probably in an effort to maintain a youthful appearance, he thought. Her hair was a dark brown but had a straw-like look from overdying. Her skin was in good condition—few wrinkles, clear complexion—and her eyes were a deep brown. Her clothing appeared clean and well kept.

"Did you check for a pulse or touch your mother in any way?"

"No."

"Why not?"

"I—I was afraid, I guess." Helen shifted nervously in her chair.

"Did you see anything unusual when you drove up to the house?"

"No, not really. There was a teenage boy who lives in the neighborhood walking down the street, but I didn't see anyone else around."

"Do you know the teenage boy?"

Helen rubbed the tip of her nose with the side of her hand before answering. "No, not really. I've just heard about him from the neighbor."

"What did the teenager look like?"

"He is about five-ten, thin, wore tore jeans and a black hooded sweatshirt. I couldn't see his face because he had the hood up over his head, and his hands were stuffed in the pockets."

"Did the sweatshirt have any markings on it?"

"No. It was solid black.

"What have you heard about the teenager?"

"That he's always in trouble. I guess the neighbor keeps a close eye on what goes on in the neighborhood. He said the police are at the kid's house a lot."

"What kind of trouble does the kid get into?"

"The neighbor said he's into drugs and gangs."

"What is the neighbor's name, and precisely where does he live in the neighborhood?"

"He lives to the right side of my mother's house. His name is Mr. Sakamaki, and he's home all the time. I guess he's retired or works at home. I'm not sure which. I just know he's always at home." Helen wiped the corners of her mouth with the tips of her index finger and thumb.

"Do you know the teenager's name?"

"No."

"Have you ever seen that teenager around your mother's house?"

"No. Just this morning."

"Mrs. St. Claire, you said at the house this morning that Mondays were your days to check on your mother, right?"

"Yes."

"Would anyone else be expected to show up at your mother's house on that day?"

"No. My brother and sister always come on their day, not mine. It works out that way because it fits into our schedules like that. Besides, none of us has much desire to see each other anyway."

"And why is that?" He shifted in his seat to face Helen directly.

"Because of the court case that's going on."

"Can you tell me a little bit more about that?"

"Well, my little sister, Carrie, and my husband had a big fight because she wanted to get a conservator to handle my mother's affairs, and my husband felt the family should handle things. There was a lot of yelling and name-calling. Later Carry didn't agree with the nursing home we wanted to put Mom in. She felt it was too expensive. That was another disagreement." Helen paused, her gaze went to the floor, and she crossed her arms across her chest. "I guess she was afraid it would use up the money she might inherit."

It was clear to Detective Chavez that animosity existed between the siblings, not only by the words Helen used but by her biting tone of voice.

"Can you tell me a little bit more about this inheritance situation?"

"Well, my parents changed their will a short time before my father passed away. Carrie gets more than one half of everything. I know what the will says because I was named as the executrix, being the oldest of the children."

He leaned forward, inches from Helen. "And what do you stand to inherit from the will, Mrs. St. Claire?"

Tears began to fill the corner of Helen's eyes. She fumbled with her purse to retrieve another tissue.

"Carrie gets one half of the estate and all the personal property. The rest of us split anything that's left." She wiped her nose with the now-damp tissue.

"That seems to upset you, Mrs. St. Claire."

"Yes, I guess so. It doesn't seem fair." Tears welled up again and rolled down her checks.

"Do you know what the estate is worth? I mean how much money are we talking about here?"

"I'm not sure exactly, but I think close to one hundred thousand dollars." Helen made an effort to compose herself.

"You've mentioned the other siblings. Can you tell me about them?"

"Well, I'm the oldest of the five of us. There's my brother, Robert, then Mary Ann, and Carrie and Colleen, the twins."

"Did anyone in the family owe money to your parents, before or after the death of your father?"

"Yes." Helen looked down at her lap and played with the soiled tissue.

"Can you tell me about that?" he asked softly.

"My husband and I borrowed thirty thousand dollars a year ago to catch up on some bills." Helen paused, wiped her nose, and continued. "My husband has been out of work for the last two years, but we fully intend to pay it back when he returns to work," she added.

"And your siblings?"

"My sister Colleen asked to borrow twenty thousand dollars to put down on a house. That was after my father passed away, and we found out about my mother's Alzheimer's disease." She paused, and her voice got slightly louder and stronger. "You should be looking at Carrie, not me. She's the one who needs money and probably would hurt my mother to get it." Tears poured down her cheeks while she fished inside her purse for additional tissue.

"Do you feel that I'm accusing you, Mrs. St. Claire?"

She claimed down a bit before answering. "It feels like it."

"I apologize if it seems that way. I'm just trying to get some facts. I'm not accusing you or anyone of anything, Mrs. St. Claire. We don't have enough information concerning your mother's death to make any accusations. However, you need to know that we can't overlook anyone if your mother's death is determined to be a homicide. And if it is a homicide, you want us to find out who did this to your mother, don't you?" He said this calmly, hoping that Helen would settle down and open up with more information. "Why do you think Carrie would hurt your mother?" he asked.

"She's very tough. She's been through a lot in her life and is capable of hurting someone." She paused. "My mother's situation has become taxing on everyone's life, but especially on Carrie. She goes to law school at night and takes care of her children during the day. Her husband left her shortly after our father died. He ran off with his secretary, and she's said many times how hard it is to deal with Mom and the situation in our family."

"Has she ever hurt anyone?"

"No, but she and Colleen sat up with guns one night waiting for Colleen's boyfriend who used to beat her up pretty badly. He never showed up, so nothing happened. But when Carrie told me about it, she said she knew she would have had to pull the trigger and shoot the guy because Colleen wouldn't have been able to do it. I think Carrie was definitely ready to kill the guy."

"When did this happen?"

"It was four or five years ago."

"Do you remember the name of the boyfriend?"

"I don't remember his name, and I don't know all the details. I just heard about it from Carrie and during some family conversation."

Detective Chavez noted this information in his mind so that he could question Carrie on the circumstances when he had a chance to speak with her. At this point in time, it was just hearsay as far as he was concerned. He decided to move on with the questioning, since it was apparent Helen was again getting defensive, accusatory, and angry. He wanted Helen to feel at ease and tell him as much as possible without her focusing on the whodunit of the case.

"Mrs. St. Claire, do you think Carrie influenced your parents to change their will?"

"Yes. I think she encouraged it, that's for sure. They would visit and stay with Carrie more than any of the other siblings. She saw my parents more than any of us did."

"Were your parents in good health at that time?"

"My father had a kidney stone but nothing serious. He used to allude to the fact that my mother was sick, but never would go into detail, even when we asked. He would say he wasn't sure what was wrong."

"Did he take her to a doctor?"

"No. His family didn't believe in going to the doctor. They felt if you went to the doctor or hospital, you never came home. That's what his family had taught him. His parents had come from Ireland when they were teens, and I guess the immigrants had different beliefs."

"So when did you find out your mother had Alzheimer's disease?"

"Carrie had my mother stay with her for six months after our father died suddenly, and she took her to the doctor toward the end of the six months. We were all shocked. None of us knew anything about Alzheimer's disease."

"Do you get along with your other siblings?' he asked as he sat back in his chair.

"I'm closer to my brother but not very close to my sisters."

"Why is that?"

"Well, there are a lot of years between my sisters and myself. My brother is four years younger than me, so I think we had more in common as we grew up. Besides, he's my only true sibling. My brother and I have a different father than my sisters."

"So your mother had married twice, is that correct?"

"Yes."

"This morning when I asked if anything was missing that you were aware of, you mentioned your mother's rings. When did you notice that your mother's rings were gone?"

"When you asked me. I looked down at her hands, and they weren't there. She never took them off. She loved her jewelry." Helen shifted in her seat again several times.

"Did you remember seeing anything else that might have been missing... say, like, from your mother's bedroom?"

19

"No."

Detective Chavez could tell Helen was getting defensive again, and it appeared that she was on edge. He was cognizant that she had been through a lot today.

"Is there anyone else that you know of that might have wanted to hurt your mother?"

"No."

"Okay, I think that's all for now. I'll have one of the officers drive you home. Thank you for your cooperation, Mrs. St. Claire."

Helen got up from the chair, grabbed her purse, and hurried through the door the detective held open for her. He held out his business card with his free hand. "Call me if you think of anything we haven't discussed."

CHAPTER
FIVE

Detective Chavez crumpled the paper wrapper from his fast-food meal as he chewed the last bite of his thin tasteless hamburger. He often had to consume a quick meal to keep his blood sugar from plummeting and his mood and attitude from souring before meeting with unfamiliar individuals. He tossed the wrapper into the plastic shopping bag he had attached to the netting on the back of the passenger seat for the purpose of collecting garbage. He adjusted the rearview mirror to check his appearance, looking for bits of remaining food on his face and in his teeth before leaving the car.

He walked up the dozen concrete steps; each step bordered by a bushy rose plant covered with large blossoms, which filled the immediate vicinity with sweet fragrance; past the white pillars of the colonial-style home; and pushed the tiny yellowed plastic rectangle located near the hunter-green shutters on the sides of the white door. He could hear the faint sound of the bell alerting the residents that someone was at their door and requesting their attention.

He heard a female voice yell, "I'll get it!" He heard feet scuffling nearby, then the door handle turned, and an attractive dark-haired young woman appeared wearing an apron about her waist; beneath it, she wore jeans and a pink T-shirt with the word Paris embroidered across the front. He saw a small, skinny light-haired boy standing behind her, hugging her leg and peeking around it.

"Hello, I'm Detective Estevan Chavez," he said as he held out his business card toward her in one hand and his shiny gold badge in the other. "Are you Mrs. Stern, daughter of Maggie Murphy?"

She took the card and glanced at it but said nothing. This response was one that he had become accustomed to. It seemed no one was thrilled to see a policeman at their front door, uniformed or plain clothed. The expensive suit, tie, and good looks didn't seem to ease the atmosphere. He was aware that the police usually didn't come bearing good news or a check from Publishers Clearing House.

"I'm here to talk to you about the death of your mother."

"Come in," she responded as she backed up to open the door wider.

"Is there a room we could go to where we could talk privately?" he said as he looked down at the little boy still clinging to her leg.

"Warner, go and watch TV so I can talk to this gentleman." She gently took her son's shoulder and directed him to the playroom then turned to direct the detective toward the formal sitting room off to her right. "We can talk in here."

He took a seat on the pink floral sofa while she sat in a beige velvet chair off to the side of the sofa.

"Mrs. Stern, I work in the homicide unit of the police department, and I'm here to discuss the death of your mother. We have not yet determined that your mother's death is truly a homicide, but I'm assigned to a case like this when the forensic pathologist thinks it might be a homicide. It's imperative that evidence is preserved and that we obtain pertinent information in the first forty-eight hours in a matter such as this."

He paused and removed a small notebook from his inside suit pocket, and his favorite black Montblanc pen.

"Please allow me to give my condolences for your loss to you and your family, Mrs. Stern."

"Thank you. You can call me Carrie."

"I believe your older sister Helen informed you of your mother's death earlier today. Is that correct?"

"Yes."

"What did she tell you?"

"She said she went over to check on Mom but found her lying facedown on the floor near the kitchen and called 911."

"Is that all?"

"Yes."

"Are you sure?"

"Yes." Carrie said as she stared at the detective for a moment with her head cocked to one side in a quizzical gesture. "Is there more she should have told me?"

"When did you last see or speak to your mother?'

"Last night. She called about three to tell me Ronald Reagan was in her front room. It took me a moment to wake up enough to figure out what she might be talking about. I guessed she had probably left her television on, so I told her to go into her front room and see if it was on. She did. Then I told her to turn it off and go back to bed and try to sleep. I told her I'd check on her in the morning, and we hung up."

"Was she frightened, or did she mention anything else during your conversation?"

"No. This sort of thing happened quite often, so I didn't think much about it. My mother would call me often with odd comments in the middle of the night or early morning. And I'm not sure she could make enough sense of the situation to register fear."

"Do you usually go to your mother's house to check out the situation she's calling about?"

"Once I did. She called to tell me that there was red stuff bubbling up out of the floor. I couldn't figure out what she was talking about, so I drove over to her house to see what was going on. It was a bottle of strawberry soda that she had loosely capped and set on its side in the refrigerator. It was leaking just slightly but enough to make its way to the bottom of the refrigerator and out the door onto the floor. She seemed alarmed by it, so I cleaned up the mess and reassured her it was okay, and left."

"Your sister told me this morning that you and your siblings had certain days for checking on your mother. Did this incident occur on one of your days?"

Carrie laughed slightly. "There's nothing set in stone regarding which day any of us goes to check on my mother. It just sort of works out that way, but no, it wasn't on my day."

"So any of your siblings or you might just go to your mother's at any time, is that correct?"

"Yes." She smiled. "We don't care to run into each other. I don't know if Helen told you that our family isn't really getting along with each other right now."

"Yes, she said something about a court action. Can you tell me about that?"

"Sure. My brother-in-law and I had a big argument because he and Helen used money of my mother's that they shouldn't have. I found twenty-six hundred dollars in a paper bag in my mother's closet when we moved her out of a condo in order to relocate her to the house she is—or was—in now. I gave the cash to Helen so she could deposit it into my mother's bank account, since at the time, she was handling my mother's affairs. It never got deposited."

"How did you become aware that the money wasn't deposited?"

"My mother's bank statements came to my address when she stayed with me for a little over six months immediately after my father died. The bank kept sending the statements here for a couple of months after my mother went back to her home in Newcastle. The deposit never appeared on the statements, and when I asked Helen about this, she kept reassuring me that she had made the deposit."

Detective Chavez sat quietly, hoping to encourage Carrie to tell him more. He used this tactic often when interviewing someone. Even when silence filled the air, he sat quietly, knowing that the other person in the conversation would become uncomfortable with the silence and start talking and most likely would reveal more than they had intended to say. In the business, the saying was, "He who talks loses." The philosophy was to let the other guy go on until he spills his guts and implicates himself. It was working. Carrie continued with her explanation.

"Bill felt I was wrong in asking the court to appoint a conservator to handle my mother's affairs. He said I was bringing in outsiders to handle a family matter. I think the real truth is that he didn't want to get caught doing something wrong." She paused and leaned forward to see her little boy's face peering around the edge of the opening to the formal sitting room. "Warner, go watch TV. I'll be done soon." She pointed as she spoke, and the little person hurried back toward the TV room. "Sorry," she said to the detective as she turned her attention back to the conversation.

"No problem. How heated did the argument get?"

"Pretty heated," she replied. "In fact, he called me a controlling bitch, and I told him if he'd get off his ass and find a job, my sister wouldn't be forced to use money that wasn't hers. We haven't spoken since that phone call."

"Is that the only time that you're aware of that any of your siblings have used your mother's money, or other family affairs that caused problems in the family?" He wrote a couple of quick notes while continuing to speak.

"No, but my mother's landlord is a close friend of mine. He told me that one day not too long ago, he was in the backyard getting a quote to put in a concrete patio for the home, and he looked through the sliding glass door of the master bedroom where the concrete was to go, and saw Helen and Bill putting gold coins from my mother's dresser drawer into Helen's purse. He said they didn't see him there."

"What's the owner's name?"

"Doug Williams."

"Did you know that your mother had these gold coins?"

"No, but I didn't know everything my parents had or didn't have." Carrie pushed her shoulder-length auburn hair behind her ear and shifted in her chair. "I need to check on my kiddos. I'll be right back. It's too quiet in the other room." She rose and left the room for a couple of minutes before returning with two bottles of water. "Would you like some water?" she said as she held the bottle in the detective's direction.

"No. Thank you. I grabbed some food on the way here."

Carrie set the bottles on the table next to her chair and sat down.

"It's really hard to talk with the children home and no adult to be with them except me. Could we do this at another time?"

"Just a few more questions, and then perhaps you could come down to the station tomorrow afternoon to give me a little more information. By then, I'll have more information regarding the cause of death."

"Okay. I'll get the neighbor to watch the kids after school. Would late afternoon be okay?"

"That would be fine. When was the last time you saw your mother?"

"Last Friday. That's the day I don't have school, so I take my little boys and go check on my mother before my older children get home from school."

"How did your mother appear then?"

"She was fine or as fine as could be expected. I was a little concerned because she answered the door in her underslip. My mother was always very modest, so this was unusual for her. I remember thinking I was grateful that she hadn't started wandering outside and getting lost like so many elderly people with Alzheimer's do."

"Did she seem confused or disoriented? Did she know who was at the door when she had opened it?"

"Yes, she knew, because I would always yell through the door that it was me. And yes, she was disoriented, but that was getting to feel like the norm. It felt like my real mother was falling off the face of the earth one day at a time and some new person was taking over the physical shell of the person my mother had once been."

"It sounds like an upsetting situation." Detective Chavez said while employing his empathy tactic. He knew if his suspect felt that he understood their feelings and why they had acted as they had, they would open up to him and share their secrets.

"Yes, it was upsetting. It was hard to see my mother fade away a little more every day, and there was nothing I or anyone else could do about it."

"Did you want to do something about it?"

"Like what? Put her out of her misery?" she said sarcastically, accompanied by a small laugh. She stopped long enough to take a drink of water and then replaced the bottle on the table. "No, I wouldn't do anything like that. I have small children to raise, since I'm alone now. I'm sure Helen told you my husband ran off with his secretary. It's only a matter of time before I lose the house, but no, I wouldn't do anything to hurt my mother." She paused for a moment. "But I'll tell you this, I've learned to believe in euthanasia, since my mother has gotten sick. It's a shame it's not legal in this country."

He noted her approval of euthanasia before continuing. "I'm sorry to hear about your husband and losing your house." Detective Chavez said with sincerity but mixed with a coldness and detachment, which he had acquired after years of dealing with the death, tragedy, and heartache contained in each and every murder case he had handled.

"Carrie, have you ever hurt anyone?"

"No."

"Have you ever been in a situation where someone might get hurt?"

She thought for a minute. "Yes, I guess so."

"Can you tell me about that?"

"Several years ago, my twin sister was dating a married man who used to beat her up and then force her to have sex with him. He would follow her around and accuse her of all kinds of unfaithful activities, even though he was the adulterer. Once he sent my parents naked pictures of her and wrote notes on them that he was going to kill her because she was a slut and a whore. The police couldn't or wouldn't do anything about his threats or the beatings. So one night my sister and I waited for him to show up at her house, as he had promised to do. We both had loaded handguns. I had been told by my friend Doug Williams that I would have to be ready to shoot and kill this guy because my sister probably wouldn't be able to do it because of her emotional involvement with him." Carrie stopped for a few seconds then continued, "So yes, I was ready to shoot and kill the son of a bitch if I had to, but he never showed up. We found out the next day that the police had pulled him over a block from her house, arrested, and taken him to jail for driving while intoxicated."

"Was there any other time you may have been in a situation that you might have hurt someone?"

She leaned forward and listened intently to the racket from the other room. It sounded like an argument between little people. "Excuse me, please." She got up and hurried out. "What's going on?" she said in a raised voice.

Detective Chavez took the opportunity to jot down some notes while Carrie was settling some dispute between her children. She returned within a couple of minutes.

"Detective, I really need to get my children fed and ready for bed. Can't we do this some other time?" She appeared frustrated.

"Sure, I understand. Can you make it to the station tomorrow? I really do need more information." Detective Chavez was reluctant to end the conversation, since he felt Carrie was letting down her guard, and was concerned that she would be on her guard tomorrow or, even worse, she'd lawyer up. He knew if she got an attorney involved, the free flow of information would come to an abrupt halt.

"Thanks for understanding. I'll definitely come down to the station in the afternoon. I can be there about one."

He got up, walked to the front door, and turned before opening it. "Thank you for your time. I'll see you tomorrow."

Before the door was completely shut, he heard Carrie yell, "Okay, munchkins, it's time for dinner."

CHAPTER
SIX

Detective Chavez had gotten six hours of sleep, more than he usually got once a homicide investigation commenced, so his mood was cheerful, and he looked well rested in his expensive suit, shirt, tie, and polished shoes. He walked into County General Hospital, went straight to the elevator, and hit the Down button. His destination was the morgue. He had never missed an autopsy on one of his victims in the fifteen years he had been a detective in the homicide unit.

The stainless-steel doors opened to reveal an office across the hall. The door to the office had an opaque frosted window in the upper center half with gold lettering stating Coroner's Office.

He opened the door. "Good morning, Sandy. Is Dr. Charlotte ready for me?" His voice was unusually cheerful and upbeat. It was amazing what a decent night's sleep could do for a person, he thought as he strode through the outer door without waiting for Sandy to reply and into the interior where the macabre procedures took place, officially known as the medicolegal autopsy. He continued past several shiny stainless-steel autopsy tables before reaching Dr. Charlotte and saw what he recognized as his victim lying naked and lifeless upon the cold metal surface.

"Good morning, Dr. Charlotte. How's it going?"

"It's going, Detective," was the doctor's short reply while he readied his instruments, turned on the mechanical recording equipment, and started by dictating the date, time, place, his name, the detective's name, case number, and pertinent identifying information regarding the female body that lay supine in front of him.

Dr. Charlotte first scraped Maggie's fingernails, letting any debris fall onto a white sheet of thin paper that lay beneath. After which, he first folded the long edges into the middle, allowing both edges to meet, and then did the same with the short edges and setting it aside. He repeated the procedure, allowing Maggie's clipped fingernails to fall into the second sheet of paper and folded it in the same manner as before. He then proceeded to the head and examined the exterior of the scalp, noting the ragged edges and bruising to Maggie's left temple. He obtained samples of her hair and skin and noted the depth of the indentation in the skull and the source of bleeding. He continued, checking the eyes, eyelids, ear canals, and the interior of the mouth, lips, and cheeks before moving on to the chest and abdomen areas. He then picked up the scalpel that lay nearby on the Mayo stand, and made a coronal mastoid incision across her forehead and pulled back the scalp, exposing the cranium. He examined the interior of the scalp for evidence of trauma and the cranium for fractures. He then cut the skull with the bone saw and skull chisel to remove the skullcap, thereby exposing the three layers of the meninges and the brain. He noted the position of the brain before removing it to examine it for injury or disease. After he weighed the brain, he took a slice of brain tissue for later examination. Lastly, he stripped the dura mater from the cranial cavity and the interior of the skull looking for fractures and signs of injury.

Dr. Charlotte again picked up the scalpel and began the routine Y incision to the chest and continued his dictation. "The thoracoabdominal incision made. No fracture of the ribs or unusual anatomical position is noted." He persisted at his work while the detective watched and listened intently.

Detective Chavez made notes in the corner of his body-diagram sheet that the stomach contents were basically nonexistent and only a small amount of chyme; partially digested food, approximately two ounces, were present in the small intestine. He knew from his years of experience that this was an indicator of time of death. He surmised that this individual had eaten earlier in the day since there was digesting food present in the stomach at all; combined with the fact that the body had been found in the early morning hours of the day, it suggested she'd been up for a couple of hours before her death.

Dr. Charlotte continued to collect fluids and samples of tissue to be sent to toxicology for further analysis, in-depth examination, and ultimate results regarding the cause of death.

Once the physical examination was complete, he removed his thick gloves, threw them in the sink above the body, and completed his dictation. "It is my opinion that Maggie Murphy, a sixty-nine-year-old female, died as a result of several contributing factors working simultaneously. The first being blunt trauma to the left temporal region of her skull, causing internal hemorrhage with contrecoup contusions apparent on the left hemisphere of the brain. The second major contributing factor appears to be a result of a poison ingested by the victim from a highly toxic substance, yet to be determined, which caused flaccid paralysis of all muscles from her eyes, eyelids, all-encompassing to the extent of the lower half of the body, including the paralysis of her respiratory muscles, resulting in ultimate suffocation while unconscious from the blunt trauma to the head and resultant hemorrhage. Upon examination of the eyes and eyelids, hemorrhages in the form of specks were seen on the mucous membrane lining in the inner surface of the eyelids, which is the pathological condition commonly known as petechiae in the conjunctivae and is usually a result of asphyxia. There was no injury or breakage to the teeth or injury to mouth or lips. Lastly, it was noted that significant natural deteriorative processes were present within the brain and had been diagnosed up to two-years-plus prior as Alzheimer's disease and were obvious at autopsy. There were no defensive wounds found anywhere on the body. Samples of hair and tissue have been submitted to toxicology for further analysis." He shut off the recording device and looked at Detective Chavez.

"Okay, Detective," he sighed. "It's my undocumented opinion that the poison was caused by *Clostridium botulinum* bacteria. We'll have toxicology confirm or deny that. However, I observed a great deal of flaccid paralysis in all the muscles from eyes to vocal cords, esophagus, heart, and all the included muscles, in descending order and equal on both sides, down to the lower half of the body. My guess is, she was fed the poison, got a terrific headache, became dizzy, and was pushed or fell against the kitchen counter, became unconscious from the head trauma, and died shortly thereafter of suffocation from the paralysis of her respiratory system. I think she suffocated from the poisoning before the head trauma had a chance to cause her demise."

Detective Chavez took notes in his personal notebook regarding the doctor's unofficial conclusion, knowing it was not part of the documented record at this point in time, but it provided him enough reason to proceed with his murder investigation.

Dr. Charlotte continued while the detective wrote. "You need to check the crime scene for signs or instruments of poisoning. Meanwhile, I'll try to get toxicology to hurry with the results so we'll have something solid to go on."

"Okay, Doc, tell me in laymen's terms, what killed her?"

"My guess is the poison."

"So what do I look for? What's an 'instrument' when it comes to poisoning?" During his decade in the homicide unit, he had not yet been confronted with a poisoning; this was a first for him.

"Well, Detective, most likely we're looking for tainted food and containers that held the tainted food."

"Is there anything else I should look for? Can this poison be purchased in a bottle or online or some such thing?"

"It most commonly occurs in food. It's a deadly bacteria, so I doubt someone is going to purchase it anywhere, online or otherwise. It's most likely found in tainted food, unless of course, you have a suspect that works in a lab where he could develop the bacteria and carry it out the front door. You'll have to look into that as far as your suspects go."

Detective Chavez slid his notebook and body-diagram sheet back into his inside jacket pocket, along with his fancy pen. "Great, Doc, thanks, I'll get on it right away." He turned to leave. "I'll let you know what we find."

Doctor Charlotte waved and turned back, grabbing his gloves to begin the cleanup of his work area and the body of this unfortunate individual.

CHAPTER
SEVEN

The uniformed policeman from the reception desk led Carrie through the open area containing ten to fifteen desks, with uniformed officers at some and plain-clothes officers at others. The chatter of the officers filled the room, and little attention was paid to a citizen being led by an officer to an interview room at the other end.

"Detective Chavez will be with you in a minute or two. If you could please have a seat." The officer pulled out the chair for Carrie, making sure she sat in the appointed chair.

Carrie sat, placed her purse on her lap, and looked about the room. She noticed a camera in the upper corner that she now faced. She also noticed the absence of any windows in the room. She wondered why the television programs always showed a large one-way window in the interrogation rooms.

She heard the door open and Detective Chavez's voice. "Thank you for coming down here today. We'll try to keep this short so you can get home to your children."

He took his seat and made sure his chair was positioned directly across from Carrie.

"Thanks, I appreciate that," Carrie said.

"Can I get you some water?"

"No, thanks. Can I ask you something?"

"Sure."

"What's the camera for?"

Detective Chavez considered this a sign of nervousness but answered with a straight face and gave no indication that he perceived her state of mind.

"It's not on. We use it when we have something to record. Today, you and I are just having a conversation, so you can relax and just converse with me."

She did not respond. She shifted in her seat and directed her attention to Detective Chavez.

"Yesterday, you told me about an incident where you and your twin sister sat at her home waiting for her boyfriend to show up. Do you remember that?" he asked.

"Yes."

"Were there any other times when you might have been in a situation where you might have hurt anyone?"

"Not really."

"What do you mean by 'not really'?"

"Well, in high school some girl threatened to get in a fight with my twin sister over some boy."

"And did that result in a fight?"

"There was never an actual fight." She paused. "My sister was secretary of the student body, and if she had gotten into a fight, she would have lost her position. The girl was in my physical education class, so I went up to her and told her if she wanted to fight someone, it would have to be me, because if my sister fought, she would get kicked off the student body. The girl backed down, and it ended there."

"So you would have fought her?'

"Yes, if I had to, I was ready to. I'd never fought anyone, so it was kind of an idle threat. Either that or I might have gotten my ass kicked." She let out a small laugh.

"Have you ever trained to fight?" he asked while smiling at her last comment.

"No."

"Any other situations like that?"

"No."

"Mrs. Stern, can you tell me where you were yesterday?"

"Please call me Carrie. I don't like being Mrs. Anybody right now."

Detective Chavez knew he'd hit a sore spot since he was aware that Carrie's husband had left her for another woman a short time ago.

34

"I took the kids to school and then went home to do homework. I go to night school, but I'm almost finished."

He interrupted, "What are you studying in school?"

"Law. When the kids got out of school, I picked them up, and we went to the grocery store, and while I was preparing a casserole for dinner that evening, I got the call from Helen about Mom, and later you showed up at the house." She clutched her purse tightly to her bosom as she spoke.

"Did anyone see you at home doing your homework?"

"No."

"Do you still have the grocery receipt from the shopping trip?"

"No. I don't' keep receipts for groceries."

"So there's no one, other than your small children, that could verify your being at home yesterday?" He leaned closer to Carrie, waiting for her response.

"No. Are you suggesting that I'm responsible for my mother's death?" she asked incredulously.

"Mrs. Stern, I'm not suggesting anything. I don't know who's responsible yet, but it's my job to find out, so I ask questions and seek information. Besides, as far as I'm concerned, everyone is a suspect until I discover otherwise." His voice was serious now. "Did you kill your mother?"

"No, I didn't. I wouldn't hurt my mother." Carrie's voice had raised several decibels.

"Okay, let's talk about your mother's estate."

"Okay."

"I understand that you are the named beneficiary who gets the largest share of the estate. Is that correct?"

"Yes."

"Can you tell me how that came about?"

"Well, I can tell you what the circumstances were, but I can't tell you what my parent's frame of mind was when they made the change to their will."

Detective Chavez could tell Carrie was getting defensive, and he decided to make an effort to tone down his accusatorial tone of voice.

"Okay, I understand. If you could just tell me how that came about, that would be great."

"They just decided to make some changes, and since David, my husband, had done their initial will, he made the changes for them. I wasn't involved in any of it. They didn't discuss it with me, or the reasons for the changes."

"Do you get along with your brothers and sisters, Carrie?"

"Some of them."

"Which ones do you get along with?"

"Mostly Colleen. Robert and Helen to some degree. Helen and I haven't argued, but I had a fight with her husband, Bill. So Helen and I haven't had much to say to each other since then." She paused. "Helen pretty much does whatever Bill tells her to do, and it's my guess he's told her not to talk to me."

"Would you say that Bill is controlling of Helen?"

"He's extremely controlling. He's called her stupid in front of the family. Which, by the way, didn't go over too well with my parents. She does exactly what he tells her to do, just like a puppet."

"Do you think Helen would do something she felt was wrong just because Bill told her to do it?"

"Probably. He rules the roost in that house. Always has. In fact, my father used to get really upset because Bill was so bossy and a know-it-all."

"You used the word 'my' when speaking about your father. Why is that?"

"My father was not Helen or Robert's father. My mother was divorced with two children when my father met her, but he always treated Helen and Robert like his own."

Detective Chavez sensed she had added the last part of the comment in defense of her father. "Was there ever a problem in the family dynamics because of that?"

"No, not really. But I do remember once when my brother caused my father some anguish when he was a teenager, but nothing out of the ordinary. My brother had been upset about being disciplined and yelled at my father, telling him he wasn't his real father and he didn't have to follow his rules."

"What happened when your brother said that to your father?'

"My father told my brother that it was he who provided for his food, the roof over his head, and clothes on his back, not his real father, who never paid child support. Then in anger, he took his hunting knife and ripped up a few of my brother's clothes. It all stopped when my father cut his hand with the knife and had to go to the hospital to get stitches."

"Would you say your father had a temper?" Detective Chavez knew the question wasn't truly part of the investigation but couldn't resist.

"Yes, he did, but he later learned to control it."

"Any other incidents like that?"

"Yes. When I was little, I was fighting with my brother for some reason. I can't even remember why now. Anyway, I yelled at him, saying that he wasn't my real brother. My mother came running into the room and slapped me across the face and told me never, ever to say that again. She said we were indeed real brother and sister and I wasn't even to think that way again." Carrie remembered the incident with little or no emotion showing.

"So would you agree there was sense of dissension at an early age?"

"Yes. But I now realize I felt the conflict or difference between myself and Helen and Robert most strongly at my father's funeral. I remember realizing that my father was gone, but my brother and sister still had their father alive and well. Then again when my mother was diagnosed with Alzheimer's. The caretaking of her started immediately after my father died. Since that fateful event, the family who used to be close and loving has totally fallen apart."

"What about your other sisters? Do you know if they felt a division among siblings like you've described?"

"I don't know. We really have never sat around and talked about it."

"Can you tell me a little about your sisters and brother?"

"Well, Colleen lives six hours away, so she was never involved with caring for my mother. She's always been kind of self-centered, so she lives her own little life and doesn't bother with the rest of us. Mary Ann has made it quite clear numerous times that she wants no part of the family. She lives on the East Coast somewhere and would probably prefer it was an even greater distance from all of us, like a planet away or some such thing."

"So to your knowledge, both of your sisters were in their hometowns when your mother died?"

"As far as I know, yes."

"You didn't mention your brother?"

"Oh, he lives five minutes from my mother's house."

"Do you get along with him?"

Carrie adjusted the purse in her lap and crossed her leg over her left knee. "Kind of."

"What does that mean?"

"I think he was misusing my mother's money too. That's another reason I sought to bring in a conservator." Carrie paused.

Detective Chavez kept quiet, waiting for Carrie to continue.

"My brother owns two houses in his neighborhood, and I'm pretty sure he was having his gardener mow my mom's yard, along with his two yards, and then paid the gardener with my mother's money for all three, but I don't have any proof of that. It's more of a hunch."

"It sounds like you were upset about that?"

"Yes."

"Can you tell me why?"

"Yes. My father worked a graveyard shift for the last four years of his career just so he could earn a larger retirement in an effort to make sure my mother would be taken care of if anything happened to him. In fact, he did so even though my mother objected to his being away in the evenings. So yes, it upset me that my brother and sister would misuse my mother's money in any way, knowing the sacrifices my father had made to provide for her." Tears welled up in the corner of Carrie's eyes. She wiped them away with the tips of her fingers.

Detective Chavez remained quiet.

"As far as I was concerned, my mother had a terminal illness, and my brother and sister were stealing from her." Carrie's voiced crackled with emotion, and the tears again welled in the corner of her eyes.

"Was there anything else they did that made you angry?"

"Yes. When we were looking at nursing homes for my mother, they didn't seem to care what sort of facility they put her in. We fought about that too. I guess it's a moot point now though, since she's never going to have to be in one." Carrie's voice trailed off into a softer tone. There was silence for a moment or two.

"Carrie, what type of car do you own?"

"A silver Subaru."

"A silver Subaru was seen at your mother's home the morning she died."

"It wasn't my car. I was using mine to drive the kids to school."

"Carrie, is there any reason someone might want to place you or your car at the crime scene the morning of your mother's death?"

"I wasn't there, so if someone said they saw me, it would be a lie."

"Carrie, I didn't say someone said you were there. They mentioned a silver Subaru."

"Well, I wasn't there. So it clearly wasn't my Subaru."

"Okay. Is there anything else you think I should know or that you want to share with me?"

"No. I think I've told you everything." She sat up straight in her chair and flung the handles of her purse over her shoulder as if ready to sprint out the door.

"Okay, Carrie. Thank you for coming down to the station. I appreciate your assistance in this matter. Please feel free to call me if you think of anything else you think I should know." He began to rise from his chair.

"Okay," she said as she hurried out the door.

Detective Chavez followed her out then headed for his desk to make notes on the conversation. First and foremost, he would note the animosity Carrie had displayed toward her older brother and sister and then recount all the other details Carrie had shared with him.

CHAPTER
EIGHT

Detective Chavez usually never interviewed more than one suspect at a time, but he needed to learn exactly what type of relationship existed between Helen and Bill. He knew that Helen worked and Bill didn't, so he decided to time his visit to their home shortly before Helen got home from work, that way he felt he could accomplish two purposes in one visit.

He parked his vehicle on the street in front of the house, walked to the door, and knocked. Bill opened the door.

"Hello, I'm Detective Estevan Chavez." He flashed his gold badge, closed his wallet, and placed it in his inside jacket pocket. "I'm working on the case involving Mrs. Murphy. I understand that she was your mother-in-law. I'd like to come in and ask you a few questions regarding the case."

"Sure, whatever I can do to help," Bill said as he backed up and opened the door. "We can go in here." He pointed to the front room to his left.

Detective Chavez noted the aged decor. Avocado green and gold from the sixties, but the furniture was well kept and in fairly good shape for its age. It would be considered vintage or antique now, he thought as he sat down on the gold-brocade armchair.

Bill sat opposite him on the green velvet couch. He pushed aside the gold-brocade pillows, which were lined up across the back of the couch.

"Mr. St. Claire, I've had an opportunity to speak with your wife, but I wanted to get as much information as possible from each family member."

"Yes, I understand."

It was apparent to Detective Chavez that Bill had expected this visit and was prepared for it.

"How long have you and your wife been married?"

"Thirty-five years."

"Congratulations, that's quite a feat nowadays," he said as he smiled.

"Some of us just get lucky, I guess." Bill was matter-of-fact in his reply and didn't return the smile.

The detective decided to get down to the real questions and set aside the niceties.

"Where were you on the day your mother-in-law was found by your wife?"

"I was here, at home. Helen told me she was going to her mother's house before she left."

"Was anyone here with you, or is there someone who could corroborate that you were here all morning?"

"Helen and I were here together all morning. We had breakfast, and she went to her mother's house and called me here on the phone after she found her mother. I guess that call would prove that I was here."

"Perhaps. Do you recall what time she called you?"

"I didn't look at the clock."

"But Helen had already found her mother, is that correct?"

"Yes."

"So Helen is the only one who can state you were here with her before she left and found her mother, is that correct?"

"Yes."

"Is there a reason you didn't go with Helen to her mother's house?"

"She normally went by herself. There was no reason for me to go along."

"So are you saying that if there was a reason to go, you might have gone with your wife to her mother's home?"

"Yes. I would sometimes go along if there was something that needed to be done by a man—heavy lifting or something like that. Otherwise, Helen would go alone." He paused and then added, "Besides, if she needed me, she could call, and I'd have gone over. We live so close that it wouldn't be a problem."

"And you didn't feel that Helen might need your company after she found her mother?"

"No." He shook his head to match the words and crossed his leg over the other then added, "She would have asked me to come over if she needed me."

"Did you and Mrs. St. Claire discuss what we covered when she spoke with me after the body was found?"

"Yes, somewhat."

"Are you aware that your mother-in-law's rings were missing from her hands at the time of her death?"

"Yes, Helen mentioned that."

"Do who have any idea who might have taken those rings or if they might have been misplaced?"

"No to both. She probably took them off and mislaid them in her confusion. Maybe you should have your officers look a little harder for them at the house instead of accusing her family, who loved and cared for her." He shifted in his seat.

"So you don't think someone broke in and took them?"

"No." Bill hesitated several seconds before continuing. "Are you telling me that someone broke in?"

"No. A break-in doesn't occur without force of some sort, and there's no sign of a struggle or forced entry at the house. If anyone entered, she probably let them in, or they entered on their own. Do you know anyone that might have come to the house that your mother-in-law would have been familiar with and let in?"

"No." He looked down at his slacks and seemed to be brushing the wrinkles from the thigh area of the twill fabric. He looked up at the detective again. "No," he repeated. "Maggie could have opened the door to anyone, I guess. She was pretty confused as to who was who. When we went to her house, we always used a key to get in, but like I said, Maggie was getting pretty confused, so you never know." He paused. "There's a gardener that comes once a week, but he usually comes on Friday. Then there's the landlord who comes by every now and then."

"How about neighbors? Do you know any of the neighbors that live nearby who might have stopped by?"

"No. Everyone pretty much keeps to themselves, and Maggie has only lived there a short time. She didn't know anyone in the neighborhood."

"How long would that be?"

"Six or seven months."

"Mrs. St. Claire mentioned that the family was looking into nursing homes."

"Yes, that's correct."

"Was there any special reason for a nursing home at this time?"

"Maggie was a smoker. She had been burning holes in her clothes and the furniture. The kids had a family meeting and decided it was time. Carrie was afraid her mother would burn down the house and herself with it."

"Did you attend that family meeting, Mr. St. Claire?"

"Yes. I am family, you know."

Detective Chavez ignored the snide remark. "Did the family agree to one in particular?" Detective Chavez knew the answer but was probing to get Bill's side of the story.

"No. Carrie didn't agree with the rest of us."

"Do you know why she didn't agree?"

"Yes. She said she thought it was too expensive. She said she didn't want any more money spent than was absolutely necessary. Although she did agree a nursing home was necessary." Bill shifted, grabbed one of the pillows, and held it on his lap while he switched the legs he had crossed. "I think she thought that it was a way to end the burden she felt her mother was putting on the family situation."

"Did she tell you that?"

"Yes."

"When did she tell you that?"

"Carrie and I had an altercation several weeks back. She said a lot during that conversation."

"Anything you think I should know?"

"She said she was really tired of dealing with her mother and that a nursing home was a good idea but that she didn't want a lot of money spent for the facility. She said she felt we could find one that was clean and adequate but didn't cost an arm and a leg."

"Is that what the altercation was about?"

"Pretty much."

"Was there more than that discussed?"

"There was an argument about Carrie wanting to bring in a conservator to handle her mother's estate. I felt that the family should do it, and we didn't need outsiders to come in to handle family matters."

"Did Carrie say why she wanted a conservator?"

"She felt Helen and her brother, Robert, weren't handling her mother's money correctly. Did you know she's the beneficiary that stands to gain the most from her mother's death?" Bill said this as if he was giving the detective a priceless tidbit. "So it's my guess she wanted to make sure no one was spending the money she might get."

"Did the conversation upset you?"

"We were both upset. There was some name-calling before we hung up. I haven't talked to her since, and neither has Helen." He laid the pillow back in its place and crossed his arms across his chest and uncrossed his legs.

"Have you argued with any of the other members in Helen's family?"

"No. Just Carrie. She's the only one who's aggressive and tries to control everything."

"What about the other siblings? Do you get along with them?"

"Yes. Robert never says much but seemed to have a hard time with his mother being so ill and confused. Colleen acted like she didn't want any part of it, and Mary Ann disowned her family a very long time ago. So no, I've never had a problem with anyone except Carrie. She really was troubled about dealing with her mother's situation."

Bill and the detective turned their heads toward the door as they heard it open and shut as Helen walked in.

"Hi, honey," Bill said in an endearing way. "Detective Chavez came by to ask some questions.

"Oh, I thought I answered all the questions the other day," she replied, looking directly at the detective.

Detective Chavez got up from his chair to address Helen. "We interview all members of the family, friends, and neighbors in order to get a clear picture of what might have occurred in these cases," he explained.

"Come sit with me, sweetie," said Bill as he patted the sofa area next to where he sat.

Detective Chavez was pleased to have both Helen and Bill in the same room. He was hoping to observe the family dynamics that Carrie had spoken of. He sat down in his seat and continued. "Mr. St. Claire and I were discussing the last conversation he and Carrie had. I understand that you haven't spoken to your sister since that time. Is that correct?"

"Well, yes, except that I did call her to inform her of our mother's death." Helen glanced over at Bill.

"Can I ask why you don't speak with her if it was Bill and Carrie who had the altercation?"

"Bill felt we should put some distance between us and Carrie until things could settle down." She glanced at Bill again.

"Mrs. St. Claire, when we last spoke, you mentioned during that conversation that there was an issue regarding a small amount of money. Do you remember telling me that?" He glanced at Bill, looking for his reaction to the question.

"Yes, that was about the twenty-six hundred dollars I mentioned."

Before she could continue, Bill interrupted. "We needed the money at the time, and we fully intended to pay it back to Maggie." He sat up straight and sat at the edge of the sofa as he raised his voice.

Helen tried to finish what she had started to say. "Bill has been out of work for a couple of years, but he thinks he's going to get a job soon."

Bill glared at Helen, "Now, honey, Detective Chavez couldn't care less about that."

"That's okay, Mr. St. Claire. I never turn away information," he said with a slight cheerfulness.

"Helen tends to get carried away. She doesn't know what's important and what isn't." He gave Helen a sour look and shook his head slightly in reprimand.

"You never know what'll be important in the long run," the detective corrected gently.

"Mrs. St. Claire, did you see or hear anything out of the ordinary when you went to your mother's home on the day of her death?"

Bill interrupted before Helen could reply. "Didn't she give you that information at that time?"

"No," replied Detective Chavez, knowing she had, but investigators were allowed to do what they had to, including lying, in order to gather the information they needed. "We didn't get a chance to cover that. I didn't feel the need to put Mrs. St. Clair through more than she had already experienced that morning. However, we always inform everyone that there will be questions that come up as the investigation continues. May I continue?"

"Sure," said Bill.

"Mrs. St. Claire, did you see or hear anything out of the ordinary that morning?"

"No, not really. The neighbor was out cutting his lawn when I drove up." She paused, and it appeared as if she was thinking the scene over in her mind, and then spoke again. "There was a young teenage boy that ran across the street at the corner of the court, but I've never seen him in the neighborhood before, but I'll bet it's the same kid Mr. Sakamaki mentioned to us in the past."

"Can you describe him for me? And tell me what direction he was coming from?" Detective Chavez pulled his notebook and fancy pen from his jacket pocket. He notated that Helen hadn't mentioned Mr. Sakamaki cutting his lawn at the first questioning.

"He was about five foot six, long dark hair, he had acne. He was in jeans that had holes in them. He had a gray hoodie on with his hands tucked in the pockets. He was coming from the direction of my mother's house."

Detective Chavez mentally noted that Helen's description of the teenager had changed slightly from the first time she had told him on the day of her mother's death. Now she had mentioned the teenager had acne, and before she had said she couldn't see his face. She also said the hoodie the teenager wore was gray rather than black. Her story was changing in several instances.

"Do you know if he lives in the neighborhood or near your mother's residence?"

"No. I don't know where he lives. Like I said, I've never seen him in the neighborhood before, but Mr. Sakamaki might know."

"Did he look stressed or hurried?"

"I don't know." She paused. "What would that look like?"

Bill interrupted again. "Does this have anything to do with Maggie's death?" He shifted on the edge of his seat and appeared impatient.

Detective Chavez's voice was slow and deliberately stern. "Well, we won't know that unless we collect all the information and evidence we can gather about the events of the morning, Mr. St. Claire. Nothing and no one can be overlooked."

"Well, if there's no one who should be overlooked, you should be questioning Carrie," said Bill.

"Why is that Mr. St. Claire?" Detective Chavez was making an effort to play into Bill's hand, since all the family members would be the first possible suspects, which was normal in any murder investigation.

"Because she probably killed her mother. She was the one that is going to inherit the lion's share of Maggie's estate, and she kept saying she was sick and tired of dealing with her mother's situation." Bill had raised his tone of voice. "And besides, if you ask me, I don't believe that portion of the will was on the up and up."

"Are you saying that Carrie had something to do with the will that might not have been legal?"

"It seems that way to me," answered Bill. "All the children were equal beneficiaries in the will before Shawn and Maggie changed it."

"How did you know what was in the will, Mr. St. Claire?'

"We were given a copy of the will since Helen was named the executrix."

Helen looked at Bill and then turned to the detective. "I'm the oldest, that's why they named me," she added.

"Would it be possible to get a copy of that will, Mrs. St. Claire?"

"Yes."

Detective Chavez kept quiet, holding his pen positioned to write in his notebook, knowing that if he did, Bill would probably keep talking and perhaps say more than he should.

"Carrie was upset when Helen and her brother started taking care of Maggie's financial matters. In fact, she hired an attorney to bring in a conservator, when she should have allowed the family to handle the matter." Bill paused. "You should be looking at Carrie, if you ask me." He stopped.

Detective Chavez continued taking notes while allowing that uncomfortable silence to hang in the air. He noticed Helen fidget, but she remained quiet. She appeared to be nervous and uncomfortable.

"We don't have a cause of death yet, Mr. St. Claire. Why do you assume Carrie had something to do with the death?"

"Carrie is broke, filing bankruptcy, in school, and separated from her husband, and she's the largest beneficiary named in the will, not to mention she often said she was sick and tired of dealing with her mother's circumstances. Isn't that reason enough for someone to want take the matter into their own hands?" His voice sounded defiant and angry.

Detective Chavez waited a minute before answering Bill. "Well, we will certainty question everyone in more depth should we find that the death was indeed a homicide, as it appears from our initial review of the scene. You do know that murderers can't inherit from their victims, right, Mr. St. Claire?"

Bill paused for a moment, as if in thought, and then put his hand on Helen's arm. "Why don't you go get dinner going? I'll finish up with the detective," he said sternly.

"Okay." She got up and left the room without a word to the detective.

"Now," said Bill, "do you have any more questions?"

"What type of car do you own, Mr. St. Claire?"

"A light-blue Cadillac."

"Do you know anyone with a silver Subaru?"

"Carrie."

"Is that the only person you know who owns or drives a silver Subaru?"

"Yes."

"Okay, that's it for now." He rose from his seat while putting his notebook in his jacket pocket. Detective Chavez was satisfied that he had witnessed the controlling behavior of Bill's that Carrie had spoken of. He headed for the front door with Bill behind him. He reached for the handle, "I'll be in touch."

"Yeah, that's fine," said Bill with an air of triumph.

CHAPTER
NINE

Detective Chavez had gotten to the office early this morning. He was feeling eager to start putting pieces together in this case and wanted to start seeing results. The reports from this case should be coming in today, he thought, as he glanced at his computer screen and noted the time. It was early, but it was two hours later on the East Coast, so it was a perfect time to call Mary Ann Melson, he thought. He dialed the number and listened as the phone rang numerous times. He was ready to hang up and try again later when he heard the phone cease ringing.

"Hello."

"Hello. Is Mrs. Melson at home?"

"This is she. How can I help you?"

"My name is Detective Estevan Chavez with the Lucerne Police Department."

"Why are you calling me, Detective?"

"Have you been in contact with any of your family members recently?"

"No."

Oh great, thought Detective Chavez, *now I have to give her the bad news.* His anxiety and stress levels increased at the thought, and at the same time, he felt sadness for the receiver of the bad news. Then in the space of a few nanoseconds, he realized he would need to be tactful and compassionate in sharing such distressing news with an immediate relative of any deceased person.

"Are you sitting down, Mrs. Melson, or is anyone there with you?"

"Yes, my husband is here. What's this about?" Her patience was short.

"I'm sorry to have to inform you that your mother has passed away." He paused and waited for her response.

"How did it happen?"

"She was found in her home Monday morning by your sister Helen, who called the paramedics. When they arrived, your mother was unresponsive and pronounced dead at the scene." He paused again to allow her to take in the information he had given her. "I'm very sorry about your loss."

She said nothing, so he continued.

"It appears to be a suspicious death, but the investigation has just begun. We have a lot to do before we can be certain."

"Yeah, well, the suspicious part doesn't surprise me," Mary Ann interjected.

Detective Chavez took note of her bitter tone of voice and decided now would be a good time to ask her a few questions. "Would you mind answering a couple of questions for me?"

"Not at all, but I'm not sure I'll be at all helpful. As you probably know, I haven't had contact with anyone in my family for almost twenty years, and I choose to keep it that way."

"Do you mind if I ask why you haven't had any contact with your family in such a long time?"

"No, not at all. My mother and I had a huge fight when I left home at sixteen with my boyfriend, who, by the way, is now my husband. She cursed us with misery and unhappiness, so I never looked back."

"So did you harbor ill will against your mother for that?"

"No. Instead I chose to make my life my own and refused to include my previous family in it. No one seemed to care then or for the last twenty-some years. Pretty simple, wouldn't you agree?"

"So are you saying you haven't seen your mother in twenty years?"

"That would be correct, Detective."

"When was the last time you saw any of your siblings?"

"I haven't seen any of that family in twenty or more years."

"Are you aware of anything that's been going on in your family?"

"No, and I don't want to know now. So please, spare me the details."

"Are you aware of any animosity between your siblings or family members?"

"No. I just informed you that I don't know anything about that family, haven't had any contact in twenty-plus years, and don't want to know anything about them now."

He noticed her tone of voice held bitterness. "Okay, I understand. But I have to ask you to understand that I'm just doing my job, and I do have to inform you that the death of your mother is considered a homicide. That means I may have to contact you with more questions in the future."

"Yeah, okay. You've done your job. Is that all, Detective?"

"No, that's not all. I still have a couple more questions to ask." He paused and knew he had to repress his temper and allow Mary Ann to give off her defiant attitude, since it might be her way of coping with the death of the mother whom she hadn't had contact with in almost two decades. She might be feeling guilt for that lack of contact, or things that were said during the mother-daughter breakup. Or, he thought, she might just be a bitch. Nevertheless, he softened his voice before continuing. "Do you know, or are you aware of your mother's will?"

"No, but I can bet you I'm not in it, and that doesn't bother me at all."

"Okay, I understand. I'll give you my number in case you have questions in the future, and I may need to contact you again with more questions." He gave her his phone numbers, both cell and office.

"Thanks, Detective. You have a nice day," she said sarcastically as she hung up.

Detective Chavez noted to himself that Mary Ann wasn't a viable suspect and his focus would be on the other siblings and the teenager, at least until he had more evidence to go on.

CHAPTER
TEN

The patrol car pulled up next to Detective Chavez's unmarked gray car, which was parked in front of Hallie's Doughnut Shop in the small strip mall.

Officer Osmond spoke into the black microphone that was attached to the dashboard of his vehicle by the tightly wound curled cord. "Detective Chavez and Officer Osmond on a short seven at Hallie's Doughnut Shop, corner of Banyon Street and Caverns Drive," he said as he radioed his fifteen-minute coffee break into dispatch.

"10-4," was the response from the female voice of morning dispatch.

Detective Chavez waved at Officer Osmond and headed for the door of the shop. The smell of coffee flooded out as he began to enter.

"Good morning, Detective Chavez. I'll be right there," said Officer Osmond as he shut the door of his car.

The officer noticed an older gentleman digging through the garbage can that sat between 7-Eleven and Hallie's. The man had oily gray hair and a long gray bread, wore dirty torn jeans, a filthy well-used suit jacket and tattered tennis shoes. On the ground next to his feet sat a clear plastic bag, which appeared to hold numerous empty aluminum cans and some bottles. He'd seen the old guy in the neighborhood several times before but had never spoken to him.

"Hey, old timer, are you hungry? Would you like a doughnut?" The officer could detect the smell of an old man who had evidently not washed in sometime.

The old man stopped rummaging and looked up with suspicion. He was used to being ignored by most people, so it was odd for someone to purposely address him. "Yeah, yeah, sure," he responded.

Officer Osmond walked over to him. "What's your name?"

"John." He stared at the officer.

"John what?"

"John Smith," he replied.

"Really? Is that really your name or one you made up?" He laughed.

"No, sir, that's really my name. Got a lot of razzing about it over the years."

"I'll bet you did. What are you doing here, John?" The officer pointed to the clear plastic bag containing what appeared to be empty cans and bottles.

"Just collecting cans. It's not against the law." It sounded as if he was assuring the officer he was not doing anything wrong.

"No, it's not against the law." He paused. "I'll grab that doughnut for you."

"Would it be possible to get a cup of coffee as well?" He smiled, showing that he was missing several teeth.

"Sure, no problem. I'll be back out in a few minutes." He turned to enter the doughnut shop, and the old man returned to rummaging through the garbage can.

"How's it going?" asked Detective Chavez as the officer entered.

"Just an old guy collecting cans. You never know when these homeless people will be useful for information sometime in the future." He sat down with the Styrofoam cup he had just filled with black coffee. "Have you heard anything on that Dudley court case?" He poured several teaspoons of sugar into his coffee.

"The pathologist thinks she was poisoned before the head trauma got her, but toxicology hasn't verified it yet."

"Any suspects?"

"Yeah, everybody, until further notice." Detective Chavez finished his doughnut and sipped his coffee. "How's it going on the street?"

"You know that teenager you told me about in the neighborhood? I remembered an incident he was involved in that occurred about a month ago. His name is Chuck Presley, right?"

"Yes, that's correct."

"I was working a night shift to cover for a fellow officer. The kid was involved in a burglary with a couple of other fellows. The report was completed by Officer Ryland. The gals in the office can pull it up for you if you want to take a look at it. The kid is really an asshole," he added.

"Great, I'll take a look at that when I get back to the office. Keep an eye out for anything in the neighborhood, will ya? And let me know if you see anything of interest." Detective Chavez stuffed his paper rubbish into the cup and got up to leave.

"Yeah, sure," he replied as he disposed of his coffee cup then went to the counter to order a doughnut for the old man who was still rummaging through garbage cans in front of the stores in the strip mall. "Talk to you later."

Detective Chavez entered his car and backed up his unmarked vehicle while simultaneously trying to watch the old man while Officer Osmond was approaching him, then drove off.

"It's glazed, and the coffee is hot and black," the officer said as he handed the old man the small white bag and paper cup. "I hope that works for you."

John took the bag and reached in with his wrinkled, grimy hand and dirty fingernails. Once he retrieved the doughnut, he took the cup from the officer.

"Do you live around here, John?"

"I don't live anywhere right now, Officer. I used to live here though." He ate the doughnut while he spoke. "I used to live in a house on Fourth Street, and had an office on Main Street." He smiled as he finished his doughnut.

"What kind of office?" the officer inquired.

"I was an attorney in this town years ago. I had a family and the whole nine yards. But that was before the alcohol took it all away." His face saddened.

"Sorry to hear that, John. Well, I gotta get back on the road. You take care now." He turned and headed for his police car, with the radio chattering away inside. As he pulled onto the street, he glanced into his rearview mirror and noticed his new friend waving heartily.

CHAPTER
ELEVEN

Officer Osmond drove the three blocks east to Maggie's neighborhood. His purpose was to talk to Mr. Sakamaki and any other neighbor he could come into contact with in his effort to canvas the neighborhood for more clues and information. He stopped the car in front of Maggie's former residence, got out, and walked to the sage-green house on the north side of Maggie's home. He knocked several times before he heard a commotion within the home. He listened carefully and, after several minutes, heard the dead bolt move and saw the handle turn before a short, slender Asian-looking fellow with almond-shaped eyes opened the door.

"Hello. I'm Officer Jeffrey Osmond." He held out his hand in a friendly gesture. "Are you Mr. Sakamaki?"

"Yes," Mr. Sakamaki answered hesitantly while he shook the officer's hand.

"I've been investigating the death of your neighbor, which occurred last Monday. Were you aware of the death?"

"Yes. It would be difficult to miss what with all the police cars and other vehicles at the house, and it was on the news."

"I'd like to ask you a few questions, if I may."

"Would you like to come in, Officer?"

"That would be nice," he said as he entered Mr. Sakamaki's home. He noticed the home was decorated in beautiful Asian decor and was immaculate.

"Come into the kitchen. Would you like some tea?"

"No, thank you. I just finished a cup of coffee."

55

As Officer Osmond sat at the table, he ran his finger over the edge of the half-inch-thick glass, which covered the top of the dark cherrywood circular table. He noticed the ornate Chinese design of dragons around its edge, the robust pedestal beneath, and the four matching chairs. Extremely beautiful for a kitchen table, he thought as he watched Mr. Sakamaki take a seat across from him.

"Mr. Sakamaki, may I have your first name for my report?" He pulled his notebook and pen from his pocket.

"It's Min. M-i-n. Sakamaki, S-a-k-a-m-a-k-i. That's my full name, but it's been Americanized. Everyone calls me Manny." He smiled and appeared proud of his heritage, both the Asian and the American parts.

"Are you the only one living here?"

"Yes. It's just me. No, Mrs. Sakamaki. She passed away many years ago."

"I'm sorry to hear that." Officer Osmond was responding to the sadness he heard in Mr. Sakamaki's tone of voice and then continued. "How well did you know Mrs. Murphy?"

"Not very well. I understood from the property owner that Mrs. Murphy had Alzheimer's disease, so I didn't talk to her, just kind of keep an eye out for her." He paused. "You see on the news all the time that these people wander off and get lost," he added.

"Mr. Sakamaki, were you home Monday morning?"

"Yes."

"Can you give me some details about your day? What you saw or heard? Anything unusual."

"Yes, sir. I got up at four thirty, made some tea and toast, then went out to retrieve the newspaper, brought it in, and read through it. A few hours later, I put on some work clothes and went out to cut the lawns. I had just finished cleaning up and putting the lawn mower away when I saw an ambulance and several police cars out front. I watched what was going on for a short while, but I had to clean up and leave for a dentist appointment. When I got back late in the afternoon, the cars were all gone. I found a business card on my door from a detective, but I haven't called the number on the card yet." He stopped and got up to remove the whistling teakettle from the hot burner. "You sure you don't want any tea?" he asked as he began the preparation.

"No, thanks. Mr. Sakamaki, did you see anyone or anything out of the ordinary in the early morning hours?"

He stopped for a moment in thought before answering. "No, nothing seemed out of the ordinary. Although, I did see a silver car parked out front very early"—he paused for a second—"but that wasn't out of the ordinary. The children of Mrs. Murphy were always at the house to check on her. The owner of the home had informed me of the situation, so I would understand the frequent visits by the children." He sat down again and placed his steaming cup of tea in front of him.

"Do you know what type of car it was that you saw?"

"It was a Subaru, but I don't know the year or model of it. There's a lot of silver Subarus around here, so I didn't pay much attention to it." Mr. Sakamaki sipped his tea.

"Do you remember what time it was when you went out to get your paper?"

"Not precisely, but it was still dark out, so if I had to guess, about five."

"Could you see the license plate on the car in the dark, Mr. Sakamaki?"

"It wasn't that dark. The moon was almost full. There was no plate on the front of the car. I don't know about the back of the car though. That wasn't the end that faced me."

"Did you notice any dents, scratches, different colored fenders or doors, any decals, fancy wheels, or tinted windows? Basically any identifying marks on the car that might have caught your attention."

He paused, as if in thought, and tilted his head to the right a bit then straightened it before answering. "Yes, the front bumper had a small dent in it."

"Would that have been the right or left side?"

"The side near the sidewalk, so the passenger side of the car."

"Did you see if anyone was inside the car?"

"No, I just picked up my paper and headed back inside. I was used to seeing a silver car there now and then. One of the daughters, a brunette, who usually had a small boy with her, would come to visit in a silver Subaru, usually on Fridays, so it didn't seem out of the ordinary.

I try to keep an eye out in the neighborhood, but I do my best not to be the nosy-neighbor type."

He sipped his tea between comments.

"Mr. Sakamaki, do you know any of your other neighbors?"

"A few." He got up and put his empty teacup on the sink. He turned the gas stove on once again and arranged the teakettle on the fire then returned to his seat.

"Were any of your neighbors out and about at when you went to get your paper?"

"No."

"Mr. Sakamaki, are you familiar with a teenage boy that may live nearby?"

"Yes, he lives in the house directly behind Mrs. Murphy's home."

"How well do you know him?"

"I really don't know him. I've seen him around and heard some rumors about him."

"And what have you heard?"

"I've been told that he has been in trouble with the law."

"Did you, at any time, tell any member of Mrs. Murphy's family that this young person was involved in gangs and gets into a lot of trouble?"

"Yes, sir, I did. I was talking to the older daughter. I think her name is Helen, and I remember mentioning that I'd heard that the teenager was always in trouble." Mr. Sakamaki went to retrieve the whistling teakettle once again.

"Do you remember who informed you of the teenager's past?"

He poured the hot water over the same tea bag as he continued the conversation. "Yes. My cousin is a teacher at the local high school, and when he saw the boy walk through the neighborhood, he told me about him. I guess the boy has been involved in a couple of gang-related robberies, so my cousin was just warning me to keep an eye out."

"Have you ever talked to the boy?"

"No. I see him walk through the court quite often. I think he climbs the back fence to take a shortcut. He always seems to be walking toward

Becker Street, which is just south of our court, but I don't really know where he was going."

"How long have you lived here, Mr. Sakamaki?"

"I was one of the first to purchase in this court, and that was four years ago." Mr. Sakamaki sipped his second cup of tea noisily.

"Did you ever talk to Mrs. Murphy?'

"No. I really didn't know her. I talked to the older daughter and her husband a time or two while I was outside, but other than that, I didn't really know anyone over there. I try not to get into other people's business. It's just when you're retired and at home, you see a lot more than you normally would if you worked."

"Yes, I understand." Officer Osmond noticed that Mr. Sakamaki had mentioned something about being a nosy-neighbor twice and noted that it must be a sore point to him.

"Did you see the older daughter, Helen, arrive at the house that morning?"

"No, but I noticed her car there when the police cars were there. I must have been getting ready for my appointment when she stopped by."

"Okay, I think that's all for now, Mr. Sakamaki. I would like to thank you for your time." Officer Osmond put his notebook and pen back in his shirt pocket and removed a business card. "If you think of anything else, please give me a call." He handed Mr. Sakamaki the card and turned toward the front door.

Mr. Sakamaki followed him and, once he exited, shut the door.

Officer Osmond heard the dead bolt turn into latched position as he walked down the concrete path.

CHAPTER
TWELVE

Detective Chavez added sugar to his coffee, stirred it with a wooden stir stick, and took it and his glazed doughnut to where Officer Osmond sat.

"Have you heard if the print fellows got anything that was useable from the scene?" Officer Osmond asked.

"They said they got some prints off the back door and one from inside the house, but nothing matched in any of the fingerprint databases."

"Anything from forensics yet?"

"Still too early." Detective Chavez stopped long enough to take a bite of doughnut and a sip of coffee. "About that teenager, Chuck Presley, did you have a chance to talk to him? I took a look at his record. He's got a long record for being so young. He's been caught in several home robberies and admits to being in the local North Side Rebels gang. I'm surprised he still lives at home with his parents."

"Yeah, me too, but it just makes it easier for these kinds of kids to get into trouble," the officer replied as he continually kept an eye on the people walking in and out of the doughnut shop. "I talked to Mr. Sakamaki, the neighbor, yesterday. I'll try the teenager's house again today. There was no one home yesterday."

Detective Chavez gathered his trash and got up to dispose of it. "That's okay. I'll try to connect with the kid, since I'm headed over to the house again for a second look anyway. Don't want to miss anything since we'll have to release the house in a couple of days. I'll try Presley's home while I'm over that way. I'll let you know if I have any luck tracking him down."

"Okay. Did you check on the silver car I phoned in yesterday after talking to Mr. Sakamaki?"

"It sounds like the little sister's car. I'll go check that out later today." Detective Chavez said as he headed toward the door, "Hey, Jeff, there's your buddy, the old homeless guy. He's headed this way."

Officer Osmond cleared his side of the table and walked over to the door to look. "Great, I'll get him a doughnut."

"Bribery never hurts," Detective Chavez said in a low voice. He walked out and headed for his car.

Officer Osmond paid the pretty young girl at the register for the doughnut and headed outside to talk to John, who was waiting for him. "Hi, John."

"Hi, Officer," he said with a wide semitoothless grin as he held up a large clear plastic bag with several items inside.

"What do you have there, John?"

"It looks suspicious to me, Officer," he responded as he took the white paper sack that held the sugary treat inside, which the officer held out toward him.

Officer Osmond took the proffered plastic bag and held it up to view the contents. "Where did you get this, John?"

"I found it at the bottom of that trash can right over there." He pointed to the rubbish container behind the officer, which stood off to the side of the 7-Eleven entrance. "I found it just after we talked yesterday. I tried to wave you down, but I guess you didn't see me."

Officer Osmond thought about it for a minute. "Oh yeah, I recall. I thought you were waving good-bye."

"Since you didn't stop, I took it with me to the church where I sleep now and then, but when I saw your police car over here, I grabbed it and hurried over." He spoke with a sense of pride for doing the right thing.

"Thanks, John. I'll take it down to the lab and see if there's anything to it. You just never know. Thanks again." He headed for his car with his new find.

Once inside the car, he dialed Detective Chavez's number, who answered immediately.

"Yeah, Jeff, what's up?"

"Shortly after you left the coffee shop, John, the homeless fellow gave me a plastic bag containing a couple of plastic bags, a stained paper bowl, a stained plastic spoon, a can with the word RECALLED written across it, and latex-type gloves. I thought I should get it to the lab as soon as possible. What do you think?"

"Sounds like trash to me. Give it back to the poor old guy." He laughed, then after several seconds passed, he continued. "So I'm assuming you think this might have something to do with our case over on Dudley?"

"Yeah, I do."

"Okay, Jeff, go ahead and take it down to the lab. Tell them to process it immediately, since we need to find out if it is indeed tied to our murder investigation."

"Yeah, sure, right away." He could feel the adrenaline rise within his body as he grew excited over the possibility of finding something critical to the case.

He set the bag on the passenger seat and dialed the lab. A female voice answered. "Good morning, Monica." He recognized the receptionist's voice easily since it had recently become more familiar. He had started dating the dark-haired, slender beauty a few months earlier.

"Good morning, Officer Osmond," she replied formally in an effort to keep their new dating relationship quiet as long as possible.

"I've come into possession of some items I think the lab needs to process ASAP. They're in a plastic bag, and I'm concerned that deterioration of the evidence may have begun. I'd like to bring them down now and have them rushed through. What's the likelihood they can get processed immediately?"

"I'll ask Burt. Can you hold a second or two?"

Before he could answer, he heard the irritating elevator music at the other end. *Why was the volume always set as if everyone on the other end were deaf?* he thought as he held the phone several inches from his ear. The music ceased after what seemed to be a couple of minutes, and he heard Monica talking to someone else before addressing him.

"Burt said sure, bring it down."

"Great, but it's a couple of items, not just one. I'll be down there in fifteen." He closed the cell phone and placed it back in its leather holder on his belt.

When he arrived at the lab, he grabbed his clipboard and the plastic bag. As he entered, he was welcomed by Monica's deep, dark-brown eyes and her full, soft red lips. He consciously adjusted his focus from the boyfriend view of her to one from an officer of the law. He felt he knew what she was thinking under her sensuous smile, since she had told him, close to a million times, that she loved seeing him in his dark navy-blue uniform, gear and all. He recalled her telling him that it was such a turn on. His hormones started to kick in, but he consciously fought to shift his focus. He gave her a wink and walked past her.

"Okay if I go back and talk to Burt?"

"Sure," she said and returned the wink.

He encountered Burt just inside the door. "Hi, Burt, sorry about the rush request," he said as he set the bag on his desk, "but Detective Chavez thinks this might be a crucial piece of evidence." He knew he had exaggerated the precise comments Detective Chavez had actually made.

"That's normal operating procedure for you guys, isn't it?" he asked. "What do you have here?" he asked as he took it from the officer and held it up to view the items inside.

In his excitement, Officer Osmond spoke up, not realizing that it was a rhetorical question. "It looks like latex-type gloves, plastic spoon, paper dish, and a can, as I'm sure you can see. I haven't removed anything. I need it analyzed right away before any deterioration can destroy what we might have here."

Burt stared at the officer for a long minute and then dismissed the comments as being from a wanna be homicide detective. "Of course." He grabbed a pair of gloves before handling the contents. "Let's take it over to the counter and see what we have. I'm assuming you need to log what you've received by the clipboard you're carrying."

"Yep, you know the drill." He followed Burt over to the beige Corian counter area.

"What case do you think these items are tied to?"

"The suspected homicide over on Dudley, the Murphy woman. Besides, it's the only murder we've had in a couple of months." He positioned himself on a stool next to the counter where Burt was using gloved hands to remove the items from the plastic bags.

Burt started his tape recorder, notated date, time, persons in attendance, and the circumstances, and continued with the contents. "We have three plastic bags, each sequentially placed inside the other, which will be sent for prints: a paper bowl with remaining bits of food particles and stained red on the interior of the paper product." He set each item into a separate stainless-steel rectangular receptacle while he continued dictating. "We have a white plastic spoon with what appears to have food particles on it, a set of latex-type gloves, and an opened can of what appears to be hotdog chili sauce, according to the label on the can, but will be processed to ascertain the actual contents." Burt stepped on the foot pedal, which stopped the tape recorder.

"Jeff, you might want to note on your report there that someone has written across the can in big black letters the word RECALLED. It looks like someone knew the contents were dangerous to one's health." He held the can toward Officer Osmond so that he could clearly see the lettering.

"Yep, I think you're right." He carefully studied the can that Burt held. "Castleberry brand, know anything about it, Burt?"

"As I recall, right around 2007, there was a huge recall of hotdog chili sauce when the company discovered their product contained the *Clostridium botulinum* bacterium. It's extremely potent stuff," Burt added.

"I thought commercially canned foods were safe?" Officer Osmond stopped taking notes. "Is there a way to tell if the contents are bad by looking at the can?"

"Yes, if the can is damaged—dents, that kind of thing. If the can shows signs of rust or corrosion, has bulging sides or top, it's best not to consume it, or even open it for that matter. You could possibly breathe in the bacteria if you stick your nose in to smell it."

"Great information, thanks. I always thought that a dented can was no big deal."

"Yeah, it is a big deal. Food packaged in defective cans could have leaky seams that can get contaminated when the can cools and spores get sucked into it. Eight to ten percent of botulism cases are fatal." Burt appeared to be enjoying sharing his acquired knowledge.

"Wow, thanks for the lesson in botulism 101, Burt." Officer Osmond gathered his clipboard and note-taking materials and got ready to leave. "Let me know when you have the results, and don't forget photos. We'll definitely need those."

"No problem. I'll get it processed as soon as humanly possible."

"Thanks, Burt. I knew I could count on you."

"By the way, Jeff, how come you're handling this instead of Detective Chavez?"

"We're working together on this one."

"Bucking for a promotion to detective, are we?"

"Whatever it takes to get ahead, Burt." He left the lab area and walked past the receptionist's desk. He tapped on the counter to let Monica know he was on his way out.

She gave him a look of fondness and whispered, "See you Friday, Jeff."

He waved with his cell phone in hand as he walked out the door. He was anxious to let Detective Chavez know what he had.

As he turned the key in the ignition, he received an aha moment. He hadn't mentioned the garbage can to the detective but now realized that all the garbage cans that sat in front of the shops in the small strip mall should be searched for any other possible evidence. His mind was moving a mile a minute trying to remember what he had read in his *Practical Investigation* book, which he had picked up and studied on his own. As he drove back to the doughnut shop and 7-Eleven store, he recalled that he would need gloves and noted to himself that he had a box in the trunk. He smiled; he'd make a detective yet, especially with this self-initiated work.

CHAPTER
THIRTEEN

Detective Chavez checked his appearance in the mirror. He nudged his fingers through the hair that hung on his forehead, until it hesitantly stayed where he wanted it. Then he adjusted his aviator-type sunglasses while simultaneously grinning widely at himself, seeking any bits or pieces of food that might be hiding in his teeth from the lunch he had just finished. He rubbed the tip of his index finger over the surface of his teeth to remove any food residue and made the decision to obtain a piece of mint gum for breath containment.

As he approached the front door of the modest residence, he noticed a worn and well-used skateboard standing on end in the corner between the front door and the wall that formed one side of the garage. There was a window next to the door allowing anyone to peer into the dining and kitchen areas of the home. He couldn't resist the temptation to peek in and noticed a small woman with her back to him, her long braided red hair hung silently down her back as she stirred the contents of the saucepan, which sat in front of her. He watched for only a second or two before straightening his frame, standing inches from the front door as he raised his right hand, made a fist, and knocked on the door. He heard footsteps inside and waited for the woman to open the door.

As she opened it, a mild, inviting smell steeled into his nostrils. Whatever she was cooking smelled good, he thought, even though his stomach was full from the lunch he had had a short time ago.

"Smells good," he said as he smiled and held up his shiny gold badge. "I'm Detective Estevan Chavez. I'm investigating the death of your neighbor who lived just behind your home, a Mrs. Murphy. Have you heard about the incident?" He noted her features while he spoke:

fair skin, freckles, bruised left cheek, small nose, long skinny neck, and graying at the temples. About fortyish, he guessed.

"Yes, on the news and through the neighborhood grapevine, but what does that have to do with me?"

"When we investigate a suspected homicide, we always talk to as many neighbors as possible. Would it be okay to come in and ask you a few questions, Mrs. Presley?"

"Yes, I suppose so." She reluctantly backed away to allow his entry. "You'll have to come into the kitchen so I can keep an eye on my stew." She led the way and motioned to him to sit at the dinner table, while she went to the stove, picked up the large spoon, and stirred the contents of the pan. She laid the spoon down again, adjusted the heat, and then sat across from the detective.

"Now what is it you think I can help you with, Detective?"

"Were you home last Monday, Mrs. Presley?"

"Yes."

"Did you happen to know Mrs. Murphy?"

"No."

"Does anyone else live here with you?"

"Yes. My son, Chuck."

"And was Mr. Presley at home as well?" He was well aware that there was no Mr. Presley at the residence but was looking for a way in which she could relate to himself and, hopefully, confide her secrets to him during the process.

"I'm divorced."

"So you're a single parent raising one child on your own?"

"Yes."

"That's difficult. I'm a divorced parent with one child also. A daughter." He hoped this commonality would assist the bonding process between single parents.

"Yes, it is difficult, especially when the child is a teenager." She played with the corners of the place mat in front of her.

"I hope your son's father is around to help you somewhat."

"No, but that's more of a blessing than a burden. It's easier when they just disappear like mine did." She paused and then began again after some thought. "Well, it's easier for me, but it's terribly hard on my son. He gets into a lot of trouble." She looked down at the place mat as she spoke.

Detective Chavez could tell that she was sharing her personal information with him and had hopes it would continue.

"Yes, Mrs. Presley, I have to be honest with you. I am aware of your son's juvenile record. I'm sorry it's hard on you as a single parent."

The silence filled the space between them for a few moments.

"Is your son home?"

"Yes, he's in his room."

"Would it be okay to talk to him, Mrs. Presley?"

"Why do you want to talk to my son?" She ceased playing with the place mat and stared at the detective.

"Someone saw him in the court Monday morning, so I just want to ask him a few questions."

"Detective, it's true my son has been in some trouble, but he wouldn't hurt anyone, if that's what you're thinking." Her voice was stern and very serious.

"Mrs. Presley, I'm not accusing your son of anything. I just need to ask him a few questions, and legally, I need you present to do so." He spoke in a gentle, understanding tone of voice, hoping that any bond they might have just formed as single parents would not be broken.

"Okay. I'll have to go get him. He won't hear me if I yell for him. His headphones block out everything except for the blaring music. I'm surprised it hasn't affected his hearing." She got up and walked down the hall to the back of the house.

Detective Chavez surveyed the interior of the home while she was gone. It was clean with minimum and inexpensive furniture in the rooms he could see from where he sat.

She returned, but instead of sitting down where she had previously been, she went to her stove and again stirred the contents of the pot. "He'll be right out," she said as she again sat across from the detective but farther to the right, leaving the chair she had sat in originally for her son.

A medium-height, thin teenager with bright-red hair walked past the detective and then took the seat his mother had previously occupied.

He slumped in the chair, his buttocks near the edge, his back curved, and his shoulder blades resting against the back of the chair.

Detective Chavez held out his hand in an offer of friendliness, but after a moment or so, he realized the teenager either lacked proper introductory etiquette or was demonstrating his rebellious nature, so he retracted his hand and placed it onto the table.

"I'm Detective Chavez, and I'd like to ask you a couple of questions regarding last Monday." He waited for a response, but it was not forthcoming.

Chuck put his large but skinny hands into the pockets of his black hoodie. As he did so, the sweatshirt opened to allow Detective Chavez to notice the printed matter on the black T-shirt below. EAT SHIT AND DIE was accompanied by a skull with a menacing grin.

"Chuck, can you tell me where you were on Monday morning of this week?"

"On my way to school like a good little boy," he replied sarcastically.

"What time would that have been, Chuck?"

"School starts at eight."

"Can you tell me what route you took to school?"

"What the fuck is this about?" he asked, raising his voice beyond what was necessary.

Mrs. Presley gave an apologetic look at the detective but said nothing.

"A death occurred on the court behind your house, and one of the neighbors said they saw you walking down the street early that morning."

"Is it a crime to walk down the street nowadays?"

"No. I simply would like to know what route you took to school on Monday morning."

"I didn't do anything illegal, so I don't have to answer your stupid questions." He shifted and squirmed in his chair. "I'm not talking to no pig unless you haul me downtown. I didn't do anything wrong." He started to get up, but the detective spoke before he could raise his backside off the chair.

What Detective Chavez really wanted to say was, "Sit down, you little shit, or I'll grab you by the scuff of the neck and haul your nasty ass downtown," but he restrained himself and calmly said, "Chuck, if you prefer, I will be happy to take you downtown for questioning, but it would be much easier if you just answered a few simple question here and now. I'm not accusing you of doing anything wrong. I just need to get some information from you to help me investigate this case."

Chuck said nothing but remained in his seat as if acquiescing to the questioning.

Mrs. Presley sat next to him with her hands folded in her lap and looked hesitant to speak up.

"Okay, Chuck, let's try again. Can you tell me about going to school on Monday morning?"

"I hopped the fence, walked through the court behind our house, and went to my friend's house on Becker Court." He looked down at his faded, torn blue jeans as he spoke.

"What time was that?"

"Eight something."

"Didn't you just tell me school started at eight?"

"Yeah."

"Were you late getting to school then?"

"Yeah."

Detective Chavez glanced at Mrs. Presley, looking for her response, but there was none. It was evident that Chuck was late to school more than just this once. It appeared that Mrs. Presley was not at all surprised by her son's admission.

"How late, Chuck?"

"I got there for second period." He ran the back of his hand under his nose and then rubbed his eye.

"So what did you do during the time you were at your friend's house and the start of second period?"

"Just hung out."

"What is your friend's name?"

"Brent."

"Brent what?"

"Brent Nelson."

"Chuck, did you stop anywhere between your house and Brent's house while headed to school?"

"No."

"Are you sure?"

"Yeah, I know where the hell I went and where I didn't go." He adjusted in his seat and pushed forward on his jeans, which appeared too big for his legs, before returning his hands to his pockets.

"Chuck, talk with respect to the detective," his mother admonished.

Chuck looked at her with what appeared to be hate in his eyes. "F-you," he spat out quietly and looked at the floor.

Detective Chavez wondered if this spiteful, hateful, rebellious teenager was the person responsible for the bruise Mrs. Presley had on her left cheek. He had noted it wasn't in a location a person would have normally received a bruise from an assault by a cupboard door or a fall.

"Did anyone see you going to school?" Detective Chavez spoke calmly in an effort to settle Chuck down.

"Well, yeah, duh. You already said someone saw me go through the court." He rose slightly off the chair and shifted his backside.

"Yes, that's true, but I meant anyone else."

"No."

"Did you go through Mrs. Murphy's yard when you jumped the fence?"

"No. It was the neighbor's yard on the other side of that house. I wasn't anywhere near the Murphy place. Are you done with these stupid questions?" Chuck got up from the chair and stood next to it as if waiting to be dismissed.

"Yes, for now anyway. I may have to come back and ask you more questions later. Thanks for your cooperation in this matter."

Chuck snickered and bolted down the hall toward his room.

Mrs. Presley got up and pushed her chair back toward the table. "I'm so sorry. He's so very disrespectful to everyone."

"I understand. Thank you for allowing me into your home, Mrs. Presley. Here's my card and phone number. Please call me if there's anything you think I should know or be aware of." He walked to the door then turned before exiting, "If you ever need assistance, please understand the police are always ready and willing to help."

She said nothing but put her hand to her cheek to hide the bruise. In a few seconds, she regained her composure. "Thank you, Detective. I'll keep that in mind."

CHAPTER
FOURTEEN

Detective Chavez stood in the doorway of his office and concentrated on the faces contained in the room full of policemen. He craned his neck and stretched his body upward when he noticed the individual he was searching for.

"Hey, Jeff, are you still on duty?" he asked in a loud voice.

Officer Osmond turned to look in the direction of Detective Chavez. "Yeah, just finished writing a report. Do you need something?" He walked toward the detective as he spoke in a raised voice.

"I just got Judge Ruby to sign an arrest warrant for Carrie Stern. Would you mind assisting me with the arrest?"

"No. Not at all. I'm kind of surprised though. I didn't think there was enough evidence to arrest anyone yet."

The two policemen talked as they walked out the locked and monitored double doors and continued down the hall toward the main entrance then headed in the direction of the officer's patrol car.

"Yeah well, it's thin—very thin, but what with the silver Subaru like Carrie's at the house in the early morning hours, her lack of credible alibi, her strong motive as the largest beneficiary, and adequate opportunity, Judge Ruby was okay with it, at least until we get the forensic reports from the lab."

"Okay, let's go for it," said Officer Osmond as he got into the driver's side, and Detective Chavez got into the passenger side of the patrol car.

Twenty minutes later, they pulled up to the front of Carrie's colonial-style home. They walked up the concrete walkway with Detective

Chavez leading the way. He knocked hard on the white door. Carrie opened the door a few seconds later.

"Hello, Mrs. Stern, may we come in," he asked in a serious tone.

"Sure." Carrie opened the door wider and stepped back several steps.

"Mrs. Stern, I have a warrant for your arrest." Detective Chavez held up the piece of paper for her to view briefly, while Officer Osmond pulled his handcuffs from a leather case attached to his massive black belt. Detective Chavez folded the warrant and placed it in his inside suit pocket.

Carrie's mouth was open in what appeared to be amazement. "You've got to be kidding. Arrest for what?"

Detective Chavez was used to suspects being surprised or, at least, feigning surprise. "For the murder of your mother, Maggie Murphy."

He began giving Carrie the Miranda warning as Officer Osmond asked Carrie to put her hands behind her back so he could put the cuffs on.

"You have the right to remain silent. Anything you say can and will be used against you in a court of law. You have the right to an attorney. If you cannot afford an attorney, one will be provided for you. Do you understand the rights I have just read to you?"

"Yes, but what about my children? I can't leave them here alone." Her voice held a tone of fear and indignation.

"Do you have someone I can call for you to arrange for their care?" Officer Osmond interjected.

"Yes. Call Elsa. She's the next-door neighbor. I'm sure she'll come right down." Carrie spoke the numbers while stammering with fear.

Elsa was at the front door five minutes after speaking with Officer Osmond. She placed her fair-skinned hand over her mouth but made no comment when she noticed the handcuffs on Carrie's wrists.

Carrie had tears at the corner of her eyes, which had not yet begun to fall. "Thanks for coming down, Elsa. Can you watch the kids for a while? They're upstairs playing. They're unaware of what's going on. Please call David at his office. The number is on the corkboard next to the telephone in the kitchen. Please, tell him he needs to come take care of the kids. Tell him this is all a big mistake and I'll be home in a few hours." Carrie's voice was jagged, and the sound of fear was increasing.

"Okay." Elsa's response was short. It was clear that she was shocked by what was occurring.

The police grew accustomed to seeing a response of fear and shock from a normal citizen when experiencing the law being administered to them rather than to someone else.

"Mrs. Stern, it's time. I have to take you down to the station," said Officer Osmond as he held her upper arm and guided her out the door and toward the police vehicle.

Detective Chavez spoke to Elsa before following Carrie to the car. "You'll have to take the children to your house and have Mr. Stern pick them up there. I've called an officer to come assist, and he'll be watching the home until I can get back here." He then proceeded to the patrol car as Elsa stood in the doorway watching in disbelief.

Detective Chavez held the back door open as Officer Osmond assisted Carrie to safely enter the car. He put his large hand gently on her head in order to prevent her from hitting her head on the car's frame as she squatted.

A police car rounded the corner just as Carrie was placed inside the vehicle. The officer inside stopped his vehicle next to Officer Osmond's car in order to get direction for his assignment at the Stern house. Detective Chavez walked around the car and placed his hand inside the open window to shake the officer's hand.

"Thanks for coming, Officer Espinoza. I need you to sit at the house and protect the integrity of the scene until I can get a search warrant and get back here. You're to allow no one into the house under any circumstances. You need to assist Elsa, standing in the doorway there, to get the kids out and over to her house. You probably should expect Mr. Stern to want to come into the house for something or other, since he'll be picking up his children. Just tell him he'll have to get by on what he already has for the kids until we release the house. I'll get back as soon as I can to conduct a search."

"Yes, Detective." Officer Espinoza then drove ahead several feet, made a U-turn, and parked behind Officer Osmond as they were leaving.

The twenty-minute ride to the station was clothed in silence, except for the radio, which never stopped chattering. The vehicle pulled around to the back of the beautiful long beige concrete block building that had been completed only two years earlier to house more people, mostly recidivists, and the enormous amount of new technology that had been developed over the previous twenty years, and to process the growing population of detainees and inmates.

Carrie watched as the huge beige metal door rose slowly to allow the police car into the garage, which held numerous types of police cars, vans, SWAT vehicles, and buses, all of which were white with blue lettering on the sides, displaying ownership by the Lucerne Police Department.

Detective Chavez got out, opened the back door, and assisted Carrie to maneuver her way out of the vehicle, since her hands were handcuffed behind her, making it hard to comfortably exit the car. "Carrie, I'd like to give you a chance to give us some more details in this matter before we take you to processing. Would you be willing to do that?"

"Yes, I guess so. I haven't done anything wrong, so I guess we can talk some more, but am I still under arrest?"

"Yes. And you have been given your Miranda rights, so you have a choice to talk to me or not. You do remember the Miranda rights I gave you earlier?"

"Yes." Her voice quaked. She licked her lips to moisten them and swallowed hard. She was visibly nervous.

"I'm going to take the handcuffs off and have you come with me to an interview room."

"Okay." She turned slightly to allow the detective easy access to the cuffs, but he motioned with his hand to Officer Osmond to come around the car and remove the cuffs.

The three went inside a dark-brown metal door, which contained a transparent window in the upper half to allow viewing of the individuals entering. They continued down a hallway and turned to the left into another hallway of mostly open doors. The detective stopped and motioned for her to enter room 105, as stated on the plastic sign to the left of the door.

"This one will do. If you'll take a seat over there." He motioned for her to take the seat at the far wall on the opposite side of a small table. He took the seat nearest the door. Officer Osmond instinctively shut the door behind the two of them.

"Mrs. Stern, Officer Osmond went to see that the video is turned on, so this conversation will be recorded since you have been placed under arrest. We need to have the tape to show evidence of our conversation."

Carrie nodded. She placed both of her hands between her legs, pulled in her elbows, and scrunched her shoulders forward. It was a defensive position, thought Detective Chavez as he watched her settle in.

"Mrs. Stern, we have evidence that points to you in the death of your mother. Did you kill your mother?"

"I did not kill my mother." She paused. "What kind of evidence do you have?" She tilted her head slightly to the left in an acquisitive gesture.

"We have a witness that saw your silver Subaru in front of your mother's home in the early hours of Monday morning."

"That can't be. I wasn't there."

"Do you know anyone else with a silver Subaru, Mrs. Stern?"

"There are hundreds of silver Subarus in this town. Why do you assume it was me?"

"I'll ask the questions if you don't mind," Detective Chavez said sternly.

"You've just arrested me for a murder I didn't commit, and now you're telling me I can't ask questions?"

"Mrs. Stern, I understand that you felt very burdened by your mother's illness combined with your husband leaving you for another woman, you're in law school, have children to raise mostly on your own, and have extreme financial problems. I could understand if you wanted to take matters into your own hands. Why don't you just let it all out?" His voice was gentle and compassionate.

"Detective, I did not kill my mother." She enunciated each word carefully.

"Where were you in the early morning hours of Monday morning?"

"I already told you, I got the kids ready for school, took them to school, went home to do homework, and after picking the kids up from school, I went to the grocery store and then home." Carrie crossed her legs and leaned forward somewhat.

"I'm talking about the early morning hours, say five in the morning."

"I was sleeping."

"But no one can corroborate either alibi, Mrs. Stern, so all that tells me is that you had opportunity."

"No, I did not. I would not have left my children alone in the house. And I don't keep receipts from the grocery store, and I don't shop at a store that has surveillance cameras, but none of that means I wasn't where I said I was." She wiped a tear that was forming at the corner of her eye with the tips of her fingers.

"Mrs. Stern, after I conclude we're done here, I'm going to get a search warrant and search your home. If I find anything at all to make our case, you'll be looking at somewhere in the range of twenty years to life in prison. Wouldn't it be a lot easier if you just told me what really happened? Maybe the prosecutor will recommend that you get a lighter sentence if you confess." His voice was still calm and very businesslike.

"Maybe I need an attorney." She sat back in the chair, uncrossed her legs, and closed her eyes.

"Okay, Mrs. Stern, this conversation is over. I'll have Officer Osmond take you over to processing." He got up from his chair and opened the door. Officer Osmond was standing ready, demonstrating that he had been privy to the conversation that had taken place inside the tiny room.

Officer Osmond leaned in after Detective Chavez had passed him. "If you'll come with me please, Mrs. Stern."

CHAPTER

FIFTEEN

Carrie paced the eight-by-nine-foot yellowish-beige concrete block holding cell like an angry lioness. How many times, she wondered, had she taken her children to the zoo to watch the animals pace unhappily behind thick bars. Now she felt as though she were the animal being held captive.

The tears of anger and shame trickled down the sides of her face as she remembered the cold metal of the handcuffs on her wrists. The cuffs had since been removed, but Carrie knew she would never forget the feeling of the cold, hard restraint of steel against her skin.

The rage inside her grew as she paced the hard concrete floor. How could they be doing this to her? It was all so unbelievable. What sin had she really committed? She knew for certain it wasn't the one she had been officially charged with by the rough, burly police officers who had processed her arrest, turning her comfortable life into a nightmare.

Why in the world would she have murdered her own mother? Her feet stomped harder upon the floor as she paced. Her body felt tense, like a rubber band twisted tightly and ready to snap with condensed energy. She peered out the semi clear ten-by-ten-inch square in the door and instinctively knew that it was unbreakable plastic she looked through and not glass. She wondered how many angry caged humans had felt this irresistible urge to get out.

The minutes went by slowly as she recounted the last hours over and over again. Her eyelids were swollen from the tears, and the rough tissues had reddened her nose. The yellowish-beige walls seemed to be closing in on her. She felt it was only a matter of time before the walls would meet, and she would be crushed between them.

A loud clang jarred her out of her thoughts. She recognized it as the sound of the heavy steel door at the entrance of the hallway. She hurried over to the small plastic window in the door, hoping that they had finally come to their senses and were going to release her. She saw only another victim.

The large female officer wearing a shiny black police jacket had hold of the upper arm of a small female with very dirty long blond hair. *Those jackets made everyone look heavy,* she thought, as she watched the commotion closely. The young girl had her hands cuffed behind her back just as she had had when they brought her in. The officer opened a large door across the hall. Carrie could see that the room was dark, had no windows, and appeared to have a thick pale-green padding covering the inside of the door.

"Put her in the safety cell," she heard another officer yell from the glassed-in control center at the end of the hall. "She's classified as fifty-one, fifty for now."

Carrie had heard this term before and knew it referred to an unstable individual. Actually, it meant someone who was thought to be capable of hurting themselves or others. It was part of the legal jargon she had learned in law school.

Before the officer gently pushed the dirty female wearing tattered clothing inside the room, she removed the cuffs. As they stood in the doorway, a very dim light came on inside, and Carrie could now see that the entire room had thick padding on the walls. It reminded her of the protective padding on the children's playground laid just beneath the playground equipment.

Playground equipment, she thought with a smile. They had called them simply "monkey bars" when she was a child, and only dirt or soggy bark covered the ground for protection then. She had loved playing on the monkey bars when she was young, but now she was behind real bars, with no freedom of movement attached. She felt a surge of sadness mixed with indignation course through her body.

The door slammed shut across the hall, and Carrie felt sorry for this apparently young but very filthy female in her padded cell. She hadn't appeared dangerous. Why a padded cell? she wondered.

She turned away from the window and realized that she had actually enjoyed the short distraction from her own nightmare. She sat on the edge of the cot they called a bed. The mattress was thin, and she had a feeling she would feel the wire mesh below it press into her back if she chose to lie down. She chose not to find out just yet. As she touched the fabric, she wondered, when was the last time the mangy cot had been cleaned, or deliced for that matter.

She looked slowly about her holding cell. That was what the officers had called it when they "gently" pushed her into it. Holding cell, she thought. *Holding* for how long? She knew one thing for sure: when she got out of this nightmare, she would brush up on the laws. "How long can they keep me here?" She spoke out loud now, knowing no one could hear her. She had been confined in this cell for quite some time now, and the solitary hours were getting to her. Certainly they didn't have any hard evidence that she had murdered her own mother. What could they possibly have found? "I'm innocent!" she yelled.

The loud clang of the entrance door disturbed her silence. She rose and hurried to peer out the plastic window. Alarm rose in her body; she pulled back and looked around the room for a hiding place. *Where in an eight-by-nine-foot cell with a cot and a toilet could you hide*, she thought. She turned her back against the door, covering the plastic so the world could not peer in at her. She felt so utterly embarrassed to be here, and now, here was what appeared to be a young adult classroom tour. *How humiliating*, she thought. A frightening thought came to her. What if it was a class from her law school? She would never be able to go back to school if she saw anyone she knew, or worse, they saw and recognized her.

Her body tensed as she listened to the voices outside. The voice of the female officer droned on with an explanation of the different types of cells as she moved down the hallway. She noticed how the officer referred to the cell across the hall as a "safety cell." *Hell*, she thought, *it's a padded cell. Let's call it what it really is.* She refused to relax her body or to move from her position against the door, even after she could no longer hear the voices of the intruders. *Intruders*, her mind recounted. *Intruders* into her world. God forbid, this wasn't her world. This was all a very big mistake. She had murdered no one. Someone would pay, she thought, as the tears welled in the corners of her eyes. Someone would pay. She felt a mounting urge to hit something or throw something. The tears flowed, and she reluctantly sat on the edge of the mattress. She wiped the corner of her eyes with her index finger and then brushed her brown hair from her face by running her fingers through her disheveled hair. She adjusted her position on the mattress, pushing on the edge of the frame and placing her buttocks close to the wall. She drew up her knees and wrapped her arms around them. She rocked slightly as if to protect and comfort herself from what was actually occurring. She wished she was in David's arms being comforted and not her own. "It's a mistake, it's all a mistake," she cried inwardly. *When would it end?* she thought as the urge to scream rose within her. She held it in for fear the officers would then put her in a green-padded cell, like the one the filthy young girl was in across the way. She had never in her life felt so alone or so deserted. Her body shook as a quick shiver ran up her spine, and she suddenly felt cold and scared. Very scared.

Her thoughts were distracted by the sound of moaning, which then turned into what sounded like a banging against the wall. She raised her head and listened intently. The banging became louder and was accompanied by an occasional scream. It seemed to be coming from the padded cell. She relinquished her protective position and tried to see if it was indeed coming from that direction.

It appeared no one was responding to the noise except her. As she looked out her small window, she could see the officers in the control center acting as if they hadn't heard a thing. The screaming and banging got louder. Carrie assumed the door was being kicked, but the padding muffled the sound to make it appear to be a banging sound rather than kicking sound.

She went back to her cot and lay upon the mattress. Her eyes searched the yellowish-beige ceiling for nothing in particular. She noticed her stomach began to ache, and she realized she should relieve herself, but she knew the pain would have to get a lot worse before she willingly removed her jeans to bare her backside on the toilet, allowing anyone to watch. *Dear Jesus*, she thought, *what did I do to deserve this?*

The tears rolled out of the corner of her eyes and down the sides of her head onto the soiled blue-and-white-striped mattress.

The screaming across the hall continued as did the banging, so Carrie closed her eyes in an effort to shut out the commotion. *How was this possible, she thought? How and where had it started?* Her mind began to recount the past few years.

CHAPTER
SIXTEEN

She was grateful her children hadn't witnessed the arrest and hoped David would be cautious about what he said to them. She knew if they were told their mother was in jail, their little minds would conjure up terrible scenes. There was no denying the programs they watched on television would assist their imaginations to run wild, allowing the most gruesome and horrendous scenes to come into their minds.

Carrie remembered a time when she was young, a time when she and her siblings had been very close. She recalled that she used to think nothing could ever happen to break up the family closeness that existed between the siblings who had chosen to stay close to each other. The fact that her older sister Mary Ann had gone away and abandoned her family had long ago been accepted by all the siblings, and the family functioned without her. It was only Carrie's mother who truly missed her and longed for a time when they would be reinstated in each other's lives. It never happened.

Carrie pictured in her mind past occasions when all the family would get together for birthdays and holidays. She recalled how her mother would go to such efforts to make the holidays wonderful. She would always go to a great deal of work to make the day memorable, setting the table with all her finery. Carrie remembered with fondness the beautiful display of the holiday table. Maggie had had a complete set of Royal Albert Old Country Roses bone china that was accompanied by beautiful cranberry-red cut glass tumblers and wineglasses. Gold-plated silverware completed the look of a royal dinner table. Mom had always made an effort to use every piece of her clear and cranberry-red cut glass collections as serving dishes for condiments and the like. She even had beautiful linen tablecloths and matching napkins. She had paid attention to every detail, and she loved showing off her treasures at the holiday dinners. In fact, she'd spent years collecting beautiful antique items long before it had become a popular pastime of the baby boomers. She always referred to her collections as her treasures. The descriptions undoubtedly came from the quote "One man's trash is another man's treasure." The children had always teased Maggie with that phrase.

Carrie recalled with disgust the times Maggie would drag her and her sister into the Goodwill and thrift stores looking for an antique item that had been overlooked by the uninformed clerks. Now things were different. Employees knew what to look for, and the treasures Maggie had gotten for pennies would now be scooped up before they ever reached the shelves that the public chose from. Carrie remembered how much she had hated the dirty old shops, the musty smell, and the old, used items. To this day, she still hated old things.

Carrie's mind continued to ramble as the sounds across the hall seemed to subside somewhat. Her mind searched frantically to discover where the nightmare she was living had begun. She recalled with sadness the call that seemed to have started the devastating spiral of the destruction of her family. She could hear the voice of the lady who lived next to her parents, in her memory, as if the event was occurring once again. Ann was her name.

David had initially answered the phone when Ann had called, asking for Carrie. The pain in her heart returned as her mind mustered up the emotions from the past event. She remembered every detail as if it had happened yesterday.

"Carrie, this is Ann, your mother and father's neighbor."

"Yes."

"Your father had a heart attack at work."

She felt fear and urgency fill her body, as if reliving the moment. "What hospital is he in? I'll be right there."

"He's not in a hospital." She had paused. "The paramedics arrived within four minutes but couldn't save him."

Silence. The man she loved, adored, and looked up to was gone. Shawn Murphy was truly and forever gone. Her heart suddenly ached, and she felt as if a small crack was splitting open and forming a crevice, which would last for many years to come.

"You're the first person I called. I haven't called any of your siblings. We're here with your mom right now, but she'll probably need someone to come and stay with her."

"I'll call everyone and then head up to stay with my mother. Thank you for staying with her."

The moment she had dreaded for years had come to pass and all too soon.

Carrie had hung up the telephone and walked over to David, who stood a few feet away. "No, no, no," she cried as she stood wrapped in David's arms. "It can't be. It just can't be." She insisted as the tears poured from her eyes onto the yellow course polo shirt that covered his shoulder. He held her close but said nothing. For as long as he had known Carrie, he had been made aware that Carrie had dearly loved her father. Many times she had mentioned that she dreaded the day he would have to die. She had never hid the fact that she adored him.

She pulled back from David's caring grasp. "I'll call Elsa. Maybe she can come and stay with the kids." She recalled a sense of knowing that she had to do her best to gather her strength since she would need to help her mother through such a terrible ordeal. It was a new emotion, one that felt foreign yet instinctive.

"Do you want me to call her?" David asked sympathetically.

"No, I'll do it. You go check on the kids, and we'll get going."

"Are you going to call your brother and sisters?"

"Yes." Carrie walked back to the telephone and paused. "How do I tell them?"

She recalled how only a few short moments earlier she had felt deceived with false hope that her father was still alive, only to have her hope thrown to the ground and stomped on as Ann explained that he hadn't survived the heart attack. She decided to tell her siblings straight out. She began dialing and glanced at her wristwatch as she waited for an answer. Meanwhile, her heart felt as if someone was trying to wring the life from it. She called the sister she felt closest to first. It was only Mary Ann and the twins that were her father's biological children, and she noted the difference unintentionally and briefly.

"Hello."

"Hello, Colleen. I hate to have to be the bearer of bad news, but Dad has died."

Silence filled the space for several seconds.

"Colleen?"

"When? How?"

"He had a heart attack this evening at work. The paramedics arrived in four minutes, but they couldn't revive him." Carrie had felt that her voice sounded strong and steady, but she recalled her heart continued to ache within her body.

"God, no." The voice at the other end shook, and it was evident by her tone that tears were also present.

"I'm going to drive to Mom's as soon as I call everybody. I'll keep you informed. Will you fly home right away?"

"Yes, I'll call about flights right now."

"Okay, let me know when you get in. Talk to you later."

Carrie had continued to inform Helen and Robert in the same manner. Little did she realize that she would end up being criticized for the abrupt way she had shared the terrible news. She remembered analyzing this in her mind later and wondering if there truly was a way to gently tell someone their loved one had died. She certainly didn't like the way she had been informed. She again recalled the hope still held out that her father was still alive, only to have the hope shredded by the next sentence Ann had shared. No, she was convinced there was no good way to share such news, at least not in the initial hours of a death.

Carrie's mind brought her back to reality. The screaming and banging had completely stopped. She felt tired. She realized that it had been this one phone call had devastated her world and commenced the destruction of her once-close and caring family.

She knew it was getting late and decided to try and sleep, hoping the night would pass quickly and bring her closer to a release from this awful place.

CHAPTER
SEVENTEEN

Detective Chavez sat at his desk making an effort to sort through his case when he decided to check with the Pawn Shop Detail to see if they had found anything in their search for the rings that Helen had stated her mother had been missing.

"Pawn Shop Detail, Cliff speaking."

"Yeah, Cliff, this is Detective Chavez. Have you fellows had any luck in finding those rings in the Murphy case?"

"No, haven't found anything yet, Detective."

"Okay, well, keep looking. If I knew who had those rings, I'd pretty much know who killed the Murphy woman."

"We'll keep on it, Detective."

"Thanks." Detective Chavez hung up the phone but immediately picked it up again and dialed the crime scene team that had handled the initial investigation.

"Crime lab cadet Cortez here, how may I help you?" The voice was young and female, but Detective Chavez didn't recognize its owner. "This is Detective Chavez. Is Matt available?"

"Yes. I'll transfer your call," the young voice said before the music started.

"Matt here. How can I help you, Detective?"

His voice was middle-aged, a little raspy but very upbeat. Detective Chavez had known and worked with Matt for as long as he had been in the homicide unit.

"Hi, Matt. I'd like you to meet me over at the Murphy home in about twenty minutes for further investigation. Are you available?"

"Sure, but what's up? I thought we had covered all the bases on that case."

"Did your boys go through the garbage can on the side of the house?"

"I doubt it. Nothing at the scene suggested that we might find evidence of the murder in that area. What is it you think we need to look for?"

"Evidence of a crime. Just meet me there in twenty, okay?" Detective Chavez had lost his friendly tone of voice and was using his "It's my case, and I'm in control" voice.

"Okay." Matt hung up, ending the conversation abruptly.

CHAPTER

EIGHTEEN

Detective Chavez parked directly in front of the Murphy residence, blocking the driveway. As he exited his vehicle, Matt's white car with dark-blue lettering stating Crime Scene Unit on the front doors drove up and stopped behind his.

"Good afternoon," said Matt as he held out his hand in congenial greeting.

Detective Chavez shook his hand firmly then led the way to the door. When he reached the front door, he began briefing Matt.

"We need to look for a can opener of some sort that may or may not have contaminated red-chili sauce on it. I suggest you don more than one pair of gloves, Matt. If what we're looking for is here, it may contain the *Clostridium botulinum* toxin on it."

He broke the red police seal at the crevice of the front door as he pushed the previously locked door open.

"You start with the metal garbage can outside, since we've already gone through the kitchen garbage under the sink, and take a look around the yard. I'll look for a can opener of one sort or another in the kitchen and garage area. One never knows where it could have been stashed."

"Okay." Matt headed out the kitchen door to the garage and then out the side door to the large shiny aluminum trash can. The top fell with a loud clang when Matt inadvertently dropped it. The rancid smell of old rotting garbage drifted up to his nostrils. He turned away and put his arm up to his nose to shut out the offensive odor.

Detective Chavez pulled on two pair of blue nitrile gloves as his eyes perused the counters for an electric can opener but saw none.

He proceeded to open the drawers below the white tile countertop, still finding nothing that resembled a can opener. He turned to the cabinet that served as a pantry. Once he had opened it, he took in a deep breath and shook his head in disgust. "Geez." He had no desire to disturb the voluminous number of tiny, mostly dead, black bugs that lay on the flowered contact paper, which lined the shelves, hundreds others scurried about. He had learned in cases past that these disgusting vermin where called *Tribolium confusum*, or "confused flour beetles," because they normally infested flour and stored grain. *How apropos,* he thought with a smile—*confused elderly woman with confused flour beetles.* He noticed them moving about inside an opened half-full bag of potato chips but did not see a can opener and closed the cabinet ready to move on to another area within the kitchen.

Meanwhile, Matt had pulled the thick black plastic bag from the metal can and dumped its contents onto the concrete walkway. He knelt down and, with his double-gloved hands, started to sort through the smelly contents. He saw nothing that appeared suspicious and nothing that even closely resembled a can opener; just normal household rubbish sat before him.

He placed the garbage back into the black bag and tied the ends into two knots in an effort to prevent the next CSI fellow from having to repeat the same distasteful task. Then walked about the yard pushing, pulling, and shoving bushes from side to side. Nothing. He decided to go check in with the detective.

"Hey, Big D, find anything?"

"Not yet, but I still have a few cupboards to look through."

"Detective, why is it that I get assigned to the lovely garbage-can duty and you get the clean-kitchen duty?" he asked in a jovial tone of voice.

"'Cause I'm the homicide detective that has the weight and responsibility to solve the case, get into court, and get a conviction, and you're just the grunt investigator following orders." He laughed. "It sucks, doesn't it?" He opened a drawer to the left of the refrigerator and peered at ten or twelve spatulas and slotted spoons inside.

"Aha!" he said loudly. "Gotcha." He pushed the cooking implements to one side to display the can opener. "Matt, would you take a couple of pictures of the can opener, the cupboard, and the drawer for me?" Once the photos were taken, he retrieved a plastic bag from his jacket pocket and placed the manual can opener in it then labeled it.

"See, you really didn't even need a lowly investigator for this search. It was sitting nicely in that drawer waiting for you."

"Sure I did." He turned to face Matt. "Do you think I'd go through the garbage and dirty my five-hundred-dollar suit?" He smiled.

Matt smiled back. A smile that said he had known the detective a very long time and the egocentric comment didn't bother him in the least; he was also aware that being a homicide detective was the top of the pyramid. "So, Detective, what significance is the can opener to your case?"

"Well, if it has the botulinum toxin on it, it becomes an important part of the case since Mrs. Murphy was in no condition, physically or mentally, to have used the opener herself, which means someone had to have used it with premeditation to poison her and, therefore, becomes the smoking gun."

"Oh, I see." Matt reached over to lock the door he had entered through.

The detective shut the drawer and sealed the plastic bag. "Let's lock up and get outta here."

"Yeah, let's," said Matt, leading the way to the front door.

CHAPTER
NINETEEN

Detective Chavez grabbed the plastic bag off the passenger seat, got out of his vehicle, and headed toward the door of the crime lab.

"Hello, Monica," he said as he entered. "Is Burt available?"

"Yes, Detective, he's in his office. I'll let him know you're on your way."

"Thanks." He smiled at the pretty brunette and turned to head down the hallway to the cubicles that held the forensic technicians of varied credentials.

He knocked quickly before entering the cubicle. The medium-gray walls contrasted the pine cabinetry with glass insets and the beige countertop.

"Good afternoon, Burt."

"Good afternoon, Detective. How is your Murphy case going?" He laid down his pen and got up to shake the detective's hand.

He held up the plastic bag. "I brought you another piece of the puzzle."

"Looks like a can opener. Are we looking for traces of the botulinum toxin?"

"Yes. I think this might have been used to open the can of contaminated chili sauce, and if that's the case, it would have traces of the toxin on it, would it not? And maybe some prints."

"Well, we'll find out. I'll get on it right away." He took the plastic bag from the detective.

"Do you have any new information for me, Burt?"

"Yes, as a matter of fact, I do. I was just going over the lab request you submitted and the glass slide from the coroner's office. We've compared the botulinum toxin we found on the items from the trash can to the contents in Maggie Murphy's stomach and intestines. Dr. Charlotte and I concur that the traces of toxin found in the paper bowl, spoon, and chili sauce match those in Mrs. Murphy's organs."

"What about the gloves?"

"Sorry, Detective, you'll have to talk to the fingerprint fellows upstairs about the gloves." He paused. "I think Kyle Kushing is the person who processed those."

"Thanks, Burt. I'll need your report on this matter as soon as possible. I'm going to need it to show to the judge in order to get a search warrant."

"No problem. I'll get these items processed and get you the full report as soon as possible."

"Thanks." Detective Chavez turned to leave. He headed for the main lobby and toward the stairs that led to the six floors that constituted the massive building. As he proceeded up the stairway, he admired the beautiful dark and light wood paneling, which had been designed to duplicate a DNA pattern. He reached the landing on the third floor and turned to walk down the hall to the fingerprint department.

He entered unnoticed and saw Kyle sitting on a stool with his back hunched and head down, viewing something through a microscope. Kyle Kushing was in his fifties with his gray hair outnumbering the black hair, and solid white at the temples. He had a round face, large nose, and gray-green eyes. Not the most attractive male, however, he was by far the most congenial gentleman to work with—your typical great guy. Kyle's attire was like his looks, disheveled but clean with something left to be desired. He wore a black polo shirt of inexpensive design, tan twill slacks, black leather belt frayed at the edges, and dark-brown loafers that were in bad need of polish.

Detective Chavez had worked with Kyle many times. His friends and coworkers had nicknamed him KKK, since his full name was Kyle Kevin Kushing, but had done so with no disrespect. Kyle had only been employed in the Lucerne Police Department for the last five years, having come from a farming community in his native state of Idaho.

He walked up behind him and spoke quietly so as not to startle him, since he assumed he had not heard the door open and shut upon his entry.

"Triple K, got a second to talk?" he said as he stood one foot from the technician.

Kyle raised his head, straightened his back, and turned on the swivel stool to see who was addressing him.

"Oh, Detective Chavez, how are you?"

"Good, Kyle. Have you got a minute to talk about the Murphy case? I was told you were probably the one working on the prints."

"Yes, I am. What can I help you with?" Kyle stood and walked to the opposite counter to retrieve his file regarding the case then turned to face the detective.

"I haven't heard anything from you fellows. What do you have for me?"

Kyle knew what the detective was looking for. He read from the file he held in front of him. "Three fingerprints and one palm print from the latex gloves." He closed the file. "However, we can't find a match for any of them in the AFIX or AFIS databases." He paused and tossed the file to the countertop. "I thought Lou Ann had called this information over to your office already."

"Yeah, she might have. I just haven't been in the office much. Too many leads to track down. I was hoping for more information."

"Of course," he replied while leaning his backside against the counter and crossing his arms casually across his chest. "Have you talked to Chet about the hairs they found?"

"What hairs?" asked the detective, his attention clearly peaked.

"I guess you didn't hear about the hairs we found inside the gloves?"

"No, damnit. Why the hell didn't that get communicated to me? It's just a tad bit important, don't you think?"

"Not sure why it didn't, Detective. Sorry about that." He continued after a short pause. "We found four hairs, presumably from the back of a hand. Only two had roots attached though, which I'm sure you know is necessary for the DNA testing."

"Yeah, I know." His frustration level mixed with anger was beginning to show. "Who's handling that part?"

"Chet Malik, second floor, DNA department."

"Thanks." He turned to leave abruptly. "Damnit," he said as he went out the door.

He pressed the small white illuminated square several times that summoned the elevator, as if the more he pushed, the quicker the elevator would arrive. As his impatience grew, he turned toward the stairs thinking it might be faster, but before he could take one step in that direction, he heard the motion of the mechanical device arriving as ordered. He waited for the slow doors to open at their leisure, stepped in, turned, and pushed the number 2 button once while the doors took their sweet time closing.

He hurried down the hall to the DNA department, entered, and encountered a young man who had a bright-red stripe down the middle of his blond hair. He looked up immediately and spoke with an urgent tone. "This is a restricted area, sir." He paused then added, "How can I help you?"

"I'm Detective Estevan Chavez, and I'd like to speak with Chet Malik about a case I'm investigating."

"If you'll wait here, I'll let him know you'd like to speak with him."

Detective Chavez watched the young man enter a large work area that was separated by a wall of half glass above and half wooden wall below. He approached a dark-skinned gentleman who had very thick black hair under a transparent white cap, a white lab coat, a light-blue mask covering his nose and mouth, clear protective glasses, and light-blue gloves. He sat on a stool and was working at a black Corian counter, which sat atop two sets of four file drawers on each side, leaving an empty area for a chair, a stool, or a person's legs while on task at the counter. There was a shelf above which spanned the length of the countertop and provided for electrical outlets and storage. An electrical cord came out of the ceiling and into the gray welded casings, which provided a frame of stability for the shelving and counter areas.

The technician turned to look at the detective standing at the reception counter on the other side of the glass wall as the young man spoke to him. He proceeded to place the small milky-white vial that he had been working with into a wooden holder and placed it inside a cabinet. He removed his gloves and mask and then slid off his stool. He followed the blond-headed boy out to the front counter and held his hand out to the detective in greeting.

"I'm Chet Malik. How can I be of help, Detective?" His accent was clearly Middle Eastern, but it was evident he had made an effort to Americanize the accent as much as possible.

"I'm Detective Estevan Chavez," he said as he shook hands briefly with the technician.

"Yes."

"I'm the lead investigator on the Maggie Murphy case, and I understand that you are the person working on the trace evidence in that case."

"Yes."

"I also understand that four hairs were recovered from inside the latex gloves and that two of those hairs had roots, allowing them to be processed for DNA."

"Yes, that's correct."

Detective Chavez was beginning to feel like he had to use a crowbar to loosen this fellows tongue. He was growing impatient once again.

"Well, what can you tell me, Mr. Malik?"

"Yes. Well, I have processed the evidence, and we should have the DNA profile by the end of the day tomorrow or the next day. The process takes three days."

Detective Chavez reached into his suit jacket, pulled out his business card, and held it toward Chet. "I'd appreciate a call with your findings as soon as you get them."

"Yes. I will do that, Detective." He put the business card into his lab coat pocket.

Detective Chavez turned and reached for the handle of the outer door and then turned back. "You do understand that I need this information ASAP and that time is of the essence, right?"

"Yes, Detective, of course." He paused and then added, "You might want to start collecting swabs from your persons of interest so we'll have DNA to compare."

Detective Chavez stared at Chet for a long moment. He felt the adrenaline rise into his face, and he felt his mouth tense in an effort not to tell Chet to go fuck himself. He didn't like being told how to do his job by anyone, let alone a DNA technician, but he restrained himself. His common sense told him he might need favors from this guy later, so no sense in getting in a pissing match the first time they met. He turned to leave, letting the door close hard as he left.

CHAPTER
TWENTY

Carrie tossed and turned on the thin mattress. The wire mesh squeaked with each move she made. She told her body to rest—to go to sleep. It refused. She tensed every muscle in her body, held the position for several seconds, and then released. She had been taught this technique by a therapist she had once gone to. It was supposed to help relax the body and nerves. It wasn't working. As she lay there, she stared up at the ceiling, and her mind once again took her to events of the past in an effort to conjure up a reason for this absurd circumstance she found herself in.

Her mind took her back to the death of her father. After the death, the next few days had moved with gruesome rapidity. A coffin would have to be chosen and funeral arrangements made. Carrie knew her mother would be in a zombie-type state of mind after losing her husband of thirty-five years, and she felt it was fortunate that her parents had long ago chosen and paid for their burial plots. At least that was one detail that didn't have to be dealt with. She knew there was little she could do for her mother except to just be there with her for strength. She was glad that her siblings had agreed to meet at the funeral home to assist with the decisions that had to be made.

Carrie noticed that Robert was playing the role of big brother and only son when he moved his chair closer to the large dark mahogany desk and his mother than any other chair of his sisters. Robert put his arm around his mother with what appeared to be a reassuring strength. Carrie was not impressed, and neither, did it seem, was her mother. None of this seemed real anyway, Carrie had thought.

She had seen her brother attempt to play big brother before and, in her estimation, failed each time. She now saw him as a self-centered male chauvinist.

Bill entered the dimly lit room and walked directly to Maggie. "How are you doing there?" he asked as he patted his mother-in-law's back softly.

Maggie turned her head up toward him. "I'm all right," she answered in a very unsteady voice.

Bill took a seat next to Helen.

"Let's proceed, shall we?" said a very attractive older woman who had previously introduced herself as Mrs. DeSilva. Her silver-gray hair lent an air of wisdom and class to her slender body and tastefully chosen suit of clothes. "Mrs. Murphy, I have several forms we must fill out. If you find this too upsetting, maybe one of your children could do it for you."

"Okay," Maggie had responded, sounding as if her mind was off in the distance somewhere. She immediately handed the clipboard she had accepted from Mrs. DeSilva to Carrie.

Carrie remembered looking over the forms, completing the information that she could complete, and making a list of several items that would have to be dug out of file boxes, such as the old service records of her father's. She had felt a sense of pride that her father had served in the navy at the end of World War II, and thankful he had come out if it alive; since had it been otherwise, she would not have been born. While she filled out the forms, her siblings discussed what words would be contained in the obituary to describe the loving human being who was now absent from the world they knew.

Carrie recalled the distance she began feeling from her siblings at that time. It was a new feeling; she had never felt separate or distant from them in the past. A different father was more than just different colored eyes, she thought. She suddenly felt displaced from Robert and Helen. Their two families lived five minutes from each and talked all the time. Recently Carrie felt excluded from this part of her family. Why had it never bothered her before? she wondered. Why was it that adulthood brought to light so many realities that had been once fantasies you had taken for granted? Now her loving and close-knit family had begun to unravel before her very eyes.

Carrie had always thought that the older children had loved her father as if they were his own. Her older siblings very seldom saw their biological father, anyway, so it always felt like one big happy family, but now, suddenly, it felt different.

"Excuse me," said a masculine voice, jarring Carrie from her thoughts at the time.

There stood a dark-haired, well-dressed middle-aged fellow holding out a large grocery bag toward her. She realized that her siblings were in the hallway and she was the only one left in the room, still sitting near the desk.

"These are your father's belongings. I doubt if you want to keep the clothes. The shirt has blood on it from the tracheotomy the paramedics performed on your father."

"Oh, okay." Carrie had responded hesitantly, not really knowing how to respond. She had not expected to be given her father's clothing. In fact, everything that was happening was new and unusual and totally unwelcomed. She recalled not wanting to see the blood on the shirt, so she dared not open the bag. She walked over to her family standing in the hallway and handed the bag to Robert. "Here," she said as she handed the bag to her brother. "It's Dad's personal belongings. The man who gave it to me said the shirt is bloody from the tracheotomy done on Dad, and I don't particularly want to see it." Once Robert had taken the bag, Carrie walked over to stand near Mrs. DeSilva, who was ready to lead them to the display room of coffins. She recalled how surreal it felt to be walking through a room containing some twenty to thirty coffins, which were displayed as if they were new cars to choose from. She recalled her conscious effort to distance herself from the evidence of the reality of her father's death. It hadn't worked. The reality remained.

The day for the funeral arrived quickly.

She recalled being at home getting herself ready, preparing the children to be babysat by Elsa, and hoping her mother was ready to say a final farewell to the man she had lived with and loved for the last thirty-five years. It was all very sad.

Once Carrie had dressed, she went into her youngest child's room, which her mother now temporarily occupied.

"Mom, can I help you out here?" Carrie adjusted the pink crepe dress to face front on her mother. Why was she having such difficulty? Carrie had asked herself silently and then also answered herself. This must be grief. It struck her odd that the grieving spouse would wear pink rather than black to the funeral, and Carrie made a careful mention of it.

"Black is too sad," her mother replied. "Pink is more cheerful."

Carrie didn't give it much more thought. There was no question in her mind that it was not her place to tell the grieving widow what to wear to her husband's funeral. She had been taught to respect her elders as a young child, and it had stuck with her.

"Here, Mom, here's your shoes."

"Thanks." Maggie's voice had crackled, and tears had formed in her eyes. "I can't believe this is all happening. He just never came home to me again."

"I know, Mom. It doesn't seem fair."

"He was only sixty-two, you know."

"Yes, Mom, I know. He was still young." Carrie had handed her mother a tissue from the box, which sat on top of the dresser, and then hurried down the stairs to greet Elsa, with her mother in tow.

"Hi, Elsa. Thanks for coming to watch the kids. I don't know what I'd do without you." Carrie helped her mother put on her soft brown mink jacket.

"You'd do it for me, I'm sure." Elsa spoke with a broken German accent even though she had been in America for almost twenty years and rarely spoke in her native tongue. "Don't hurry home, the children and I will be fine."

David, Carrie, and Maggie had hurried out the door, since Maggie had expressed a desire to view her deceased husband before anyone else arrived.

They pulled into the parking lot where Helen and Bill waited for Maggie to arrive. *They were always the first to arrive anywhere,* Carrie remembered thinking.

Maggie now had shifted the dependency she had always laid upon her husband's shoulders to Carrie. She followed Carrie's advice and instructions for everything. Carrie knew that once the siblings realized that Maggie's dependence had shifted to Carrie, the realization would cause emotions to flare, but she didn't care since it was she who had taken in her mother for the foreseeable future when no one else had offered or suggested they share the burden.

Carrie recalled the services were short and pleasant and the sun had warmed the atmosphere at the cemetery, making the mood a little less morose. Maggie had been pleased by the amount of people who had attended in order to pay their final respects to such a fine man. The fragrance of the many floral bouquets filled the air, making the scent pleasing to the senses and uplifting to the heart.

Carrie recalled the feeling of relief that the final farewell was over, and wondering what the future would hold for this family.

CHAPTER
TWENTY-ONE

Carrie had fallen asleep for what seemed a very short time when she was awakened by the banging and screaming from the padded cell across the hall. She rubbed her forehead with the tips of her fingers in an effort to erase the headache she felt coming on from the lack of sleep.

She heard heavy footsteps coming down the hall but didn't bother to get up to see what was going on. Then the banging grew louder. It sounded like the guard slamming her nightstick against the door of the padded cell.

"Quiet down in there, or we'll have to use the largest hypodermic needle we have to settle you down," said a deep female voice, putting emphasis on the word *largest*. "How would you like that?" the voice taunted.

The screaming and banging stopped.

"You're not as dumb as they told me you were, are you, honey?" The officer's heavy steps went back up the hall, and the heavy metal entry door closed with a clang.

The silence once again allowed Carrie's mind to take full advantage by forcefully leading her back down the path of memories of her father's death.

She recalled that five days after his funeral, Maggie could not stop remarking to Carrie or anyone who would listen that the man she had spent thirty-five years with had gone to work and had simply never come home.

It was clear that someone would have to go to Maggie's house and clear out Shawn's clothing, since Maggie had told Carrie she didn't think she could deal with that aspect of Shawn's death. When Carrie discussed it with David, he made it clear he was reluctant to stay at home with his mother-in-law and the children but said he understood. He also made it clear to Carrie that he was doing so only in the hope that Maggie would be able to return to her home sooner rather than later.

Carrie remembered with clarity that she and Robert had driven to Newcastle together to complete the task, and the events that had taken place.

"It's so hard to believe that Dad's gone," Robert said while driving.

"Yeah, I know. It was all so sudden. I guess in a way that's good. At least he didn't have to suffer."

"That's true. That part is left for us to do," he replied with a tone of resentment.

Carrie remembered that she felt her own degree of resentment. She had not yet acknowledged it from within and wasn't sure then what she was resentful about, but it was there nevertheless. She had made an effort to change the subject.

"Do you think anyone will want to use anything of Dad's?"

"I don't, but I can't speak for anyone else."

"I think we should put everything in boxes and put it in my garage until everyone has had a chance to take whatever they want. We'll give whatever is left to Goodwill."

"That's a good idea." Robert said as he put his window down slightly to let in fresh air.

They had taken Carrie's yellow Ford station wagon, since she knew that Robert wouldn't allow his precious Shelby Mustang to be used as a moving van. He had worked many hours fixing it up and spent tons of money for its shiny black metal-flaked paint job.

Once they arrived in town, they had gathered boxes from behind several grocery stores then headed toward the house that had so recently been filled with love and life of a man and woman but now held only silence and heartache.

Carrie remembered she had been the first to walk in. She opened the curtains hoping to allow the light to spread some cheerfulness to the lonely house. She paused for a moment at the window, noticing the garden out back, which her father had so lovingly attended year after year. She recalled with sadness how he used to bring bags of fresh vegetables and fruits when they came down to have dinner at her home." Tears formed in her eyes. She wiped them away, turned to Robert, and said, "Let's get started."

"Where do you want to start?"

"Let's start with the closet in the master bedroom." She wiped the remaining tears from her eyes and led the way up the stairs, followed by Robert, who was holding several boxes, which he set down at the top of the stairs.

"I'll get more boxes. You go ahead and start," Robert had said.

Carrie had wondered at the time if Robert was afraid or superstitious about handling their deceased father's clothing. She sensed that he was acting strange.

"Okay," she replied as he headed down the stairs while she opened the mirrored closet door. She stepped in and began neatly folding each piece of her father's clothing and placing them in the boxes. The scent on several of the shirts brought the memory of the person she loved most back to life. She recalled how she had first become acquainted with this scent; it was when she was a young girl ironing the family clothes to increase her allowance funds. Her father's shirts held his scent in a gentle way, not at all displeasing, but the scent remained in her memory banks for many years. She held the shirt lovingly to her face, taking in the living smell of her late father.

Robert's voice shattered her loving thoughts of her father and forced her mind to the task at hand. "Is that enough boxes?"

"Yes, that's enough for this closet anyway. Mom requested that we be sure to remove Dad's guns from the house. She said they would be in the pink room."

"I'll get them," Robert responded anxiously.

He had never hunted in his life, Carrie remembered thinking. It seemed odd that he was so anxious to handle the guns but not the clothing.

"What else needs to be done?" Robert asked when he returned from the pink room.

"You can start packing up Dad's clothes in the dresser drawers."

"How about I start taking the full boxes downstairs instead?"

Carrie watched him for a long moment. Robert was an attractive man. The soft full head of dark-brown hair, the smooth well-sculpted features of his face—he seemed so gentle. He could have passed for an Elvis Presley look-alike. He had never expressed any extreme masculinity, but neither was he a sissy of any sort. What was this reluctance to touch his step-father's clothing? she wondered. Fear or superstition, she had thought. Then dismissing the idea, she turned back to the task.

All the boxes had been packed and placed in the back of Carrie's car. The only things left inside were the four rifles and one old handgun.

"I guess we might as well divide these up," Robert said as he reached for one of the rifles.

"Okay. I guess one to each of the kids. Why don't you choose first since you're the only son."

"Okay." Robert looked over each weapon carefully and chose the best. It was a thirty-odd-six with a high-powered scope. He picked up another. "This is a duck gun. You've shot duck before, haven't you?"

"No, but Colleen has. Let's see that she gets that one."

"Okay, which one do you want?"

"I don't know. I'll give it some thought before we divide up the rest."

"Okay, let's head home, shall we? Oh, by the way, I took Dad's tools since I didn't think anyone else would use them."

"Sure, Robert. You're the only one who owns gas stations, so I'm sure you'll use them more than any of the rest of us." Carrie had wondered if Robert could detect the resentment she was feeling. Robert had caused her father nothing but hell in his teenage years, and now he was playing the dutiful, loving son who wanted part of what her father had been. Maybe she was being unfair, she thought, but Carrie again felt the distancing that was taking place between her and her siblings.

CHAPTER
TWENTY-TWO

She was awakened by loud banging on her door.

"Get up. Gotta go to court!" yelled a husky female voice. "You got ten minutes to pretty up." The officer opened the door and threw in an orange jumpsuit, which landed near the bed. "Put 'em on," she said as she shut the door.

Carrie sat up. She looked around at the strange surroundings, then her stomach turned as she recalled where she was and what had occurred the previous day. She washed her face in the small basin above and to the side of the stainless-steel toilet when her bladder demanded to burst if not relieved. She reluctantly pulled down her stonewashed blue jeans and peed.

"Wow." That felt so much better, she thought.

Carrie picked up the jumpsuit and attempted to put it on when she noticed the words DOC and, underneath it, Dept. of Corrections in huge black letters across the back. Her stomach turned, and she felt suddenly hot and nauseated.

"Want some breakfast?" yelled the same voice as earlier. A small round, fat pale-white face with a red bulbous nose pushed against the window.

"No. No, thank you." Carrie answered instinctively. She wanted as little of this place as possible. Once dressed, she sat on the edge of the cot and waited for the next demand. She hoped David would be there in court with an attorney. He'd get her out of this mess. He must know she needed an attorney even though she had not had a chance to talk to him since her arrest.

Her eyes scanned the walls as she sat waiting. *At least, it's well painted*, she thought. *Our good ol' tax dollars at work, I guess. Gotta keep up the county jails.* She noticed she no longer felt like the walls would move in and crush her. The bright lights felt better this morning as well, but she longed for the real sunlight outside to warm her inner core. She felt more optimistic that today she would be released from this nightmare.

The door opened, and the short, heavy guard who had offered breakfast was now instructing her to enter the hallway and to bring her clothes with her. The guard led half a dozen women of varied ages to the glassed-in control center and instructed them to stop in the open area and wait there. Another guard came from inside the control center with several large clear bags that read INMATE PERSONAL BELONGINGS on one side.

"Drop your things in the bag when I hold it open for you. I'll give you a permanent marker to sign your name on the bag. Make it legible, or you won't get your belongings back when the time comes." Her voice was very matter-of-fact, with no emotion and no hint of compassion for the women who stood in front of her.

All six females had deposited their personal items and were now being led by Ms. Piggy, as Carrie had nicknamed her. It wasn't a nice nickname to be sure, but right now, Carrie wasn't feeling like a politically correct, nice little lady. She was beginning to feel like part of the chain gang being led out to the rock pile. No one had informed the detainees where they were going or how they would get there; they only received short, definite instructions every thirty feet or so. The voice in her head was singing, *You're in the army now. You'll never get rich by digging a ditch. You're in the army now.*

"Hands forward, ladies!" yelled the short, fat, white officer.

Carrie winced at the sound of the cold metal handcuffs being closed onto their wrists as each female received her shiny pair of silver bracelets. A door opened to the outside. The sun was bright and warm. She turned the corner and saw the large white-and-blue bus. She noticed that the windows were opaque from this side, but Carrie hoped she would be able to see out once she entered the bus.

"This is your transport to the court, so sit and enjoy the entertainment for now," said Ms. Piggy as she swung her baton and stood at the door directing the females out the door and into the bus. Carrie wondered if this diminutive individual was ever forced to use the baton, and assumed with her size and shape, she probably didn't pose much of a threat to anyone. It seemed amazing that a uniform and a silver badge would give someone this size a feeling of authority and control over others much larger, and probably stronger, than she. The mere fact that her five-foot-by-three-foot frame would most likely prevent her from making the smallest of defensive moves seemed incredible. All of a sudden, Carrie felt sorry for this disillusioned soul. Maybe I shouldn't nickname her. *Nah*, she thought, *I need some type of amusement to survive this place.* She stepped up into the bus and chose a seat near the front.

The bus was started up by a young male gentleman with the all-too-familiar beige officer's uniform on. He nodded to Ms. Piggy as she and another officer boarded the bus. He put it into gear, and it chugged alongside the long chain-link fence, which had circular barbed razor wire along the top of it. The mean-looking razor barbs stuck out menacingly in warning and stretched out the full length of the fencing. About a hundred and ninety feet in front of the bus stood a huge chain-link gate, which slowly moved to one side, allowing the bus to exit the prison grounds.

As she watched the prison yard pass outside the window, she suddenly thought of the death penalty. She had always been so dogmatic about her beliefs, but now she was feeling unsure of everything she had ever come to believe. She now understood how an innocent person could easily be framed for something they had never done and, perhaps, convicted and executed wrongly. Her view of the world was changing with each minute she spent dwelling in her own personal nightmare. She prayed silently that this was not going to be one of those circumstances and that God would deliver her home safely to her children.

What, in God's name, could they have against her? she thought. The silver Subaru—shit, everybody had a silver Subaru. Prints—sure, why not? She was at her mother's house on a weekly basis. Alibi—well, okay, she didn't have anyone to corroborate her story, but that was her story, and she was sticking to it. Anyway, it was the truth. An idea popped into her head. She would agree to take a polygraph. Yeah, that would prove she wasn't lying. At least, it was sure worth a try. She realized she needed an attorney. Her need to see David in court with an attorney sitting next to him, waiting to talk to her, was growing stronger with every minute. She silently watched as the cars drove on the left side of the bus along the busy highway. She hoped the trip to court wouldn't be long. She wanted out of this, and she wanted out now.

She recounted the past in her mind. How many times had she said out loud that her mother would be better off dead? "My God," she whispered to herself. Surely, people understood what she meant when she said that. Her mother had no quality of life. Who in the world would want to live on under those circumstances? Her mother didn't know her own family most of the time. She wasn't eating correctly, couldn't dress herself, didn't realize the people on television were one-dimensional and not in real time. She was burning holes in her clothing and in the furniture with her cigarettes, which she'd stop really enjoying years ago. *For Pete's sake, she couldn't even wipe her ass with any accuracy,* thought Carrie, as she remembered seeing dried black stuff under her mother's long fingernails and later realizing what it was that lay at the tips of her fingers.

The bus rumbled into the parking lot of the courthouse and next to a side entrance. Ms. Piggy was the first to step out.

"Come on," she yelled, "let's get going!"

Thank goodness, thought Carrie, David would be there with an attorney, she was sure of it. She'd remember to tell him the officers neglected to instruct the busload of females to sing "Kum Ba Yah" during the trip over. She smiled quickly, enjoying her own bit of comic relief.

As she entered the courtroom, her eyes searched the room to find David. She looked carefully and then looked again, more slowly the second time, while trying to calm herself and ease the fear she was feeling.

She took a seat in one of the front chairs, which were normally reserved for the jury, as instructed by the court bailiff. She felt nauseated but wondered why she felt sick, since she had no food in her belly, having refused breakfast. She heard her name called. She stood but hesitated to move forward.

"Come forward, Mrs. Stern," said the female judge. "I don't bite."

"Yes, Your Honor." Carrie stepped out of the jury box and made her way to the front of the judge's bench.

"You are here for your first advisement, Mrs. Stern. Are you aware of that?" The judge spoke respectfully with a beautiful Southern accent.

"Yes, Your Honor. I am aware of the judicial system." Carrie noticed the judge tilted her head and glared at her. Carrie hoped she hadn't sounded disrespectful. "I'm a law student and have been to court many times to watch different proceedings," she explained.

"Mrs. Stern, are you represented by an attorney?"

"My husband should be here with an attorney, Your Honor." Carrie began to shake slightly.

"Well, look around, my dear. Do you see your husband and an attorney in the courtroom?"

She turned to take another glance of those persons who occupied the room and then turned back toward the judge. "No, Your Honor."

"Well, I've reviewed your file and the documentation produced by the district attorney's office. I have reason to believe that there is probable cause for your arrest for the murder of Mrs. Murphy. I believe it to be sufficient, and I am ready to order that you be held until such time as the district attorney's office files formal charges. Do you have anything to say, Mrs. Stern?"

"My husband sho-should be here." Fear was evident in her voice.

The judge ignored her comment and continued. "Mrs. Stern, murder is a pretty serious charge. I suggest that when you get transferred back to the detention center, you make a phone call or two. Or would you like me to appoint a public defender to take your case?"

"No, Your Honor. I'll get an attorney."

"All right then. I am ordering you be held for the minimum of seventy-two hours, with no bond. Return to your seat, Mrs. Stern."

Carrie was aware that she probably should say "Thank you, Your Honor" but lacked the desire to follow proper court protocol at this moment. Her fear seemed to take priority of her feelings, so she took her seat as instructed and waited for the other detainees to complete their advisements.

CHAPTER
TWENTY-THREE

As the door opened in response to his knock, the detective held his badge ready to show to the occupant.

A small blond lady opened the door but said nothing.

"Hello, I'm Detective Estevan Chavez, and I'm investigating the Maggie Murphy homicide. May I ask who you are?"

"I'm Kathy Mulligan. Who were you looking for?"

Detective Chavez was taken aback for a moment as she spoke. Her voice was as tiny as she was and had a squeaky, mousy quality to it, as if from a toy doll.

"I'm here to talk to Robert Mulligan about his mother's death." He waited for her to open the screen door and invite him in, but to no avail. She left him standing on the other side of the door.

"I'll let him know you're here and that you wish to speak with him," she squeaked out and then turned to deliver the message.

As he stood at the door waiting, he surveyed his surroundings. He noted the yard was well manicured, and saw a small sixteen-foot catamaran that sat off to the side of the yard on a concrete pad, which appeared to have been poured for the purpose of storing the boat. The neighborhood appeared quiet, and all the yards were well-kept.

He heard footsteps and then a voice. He turned to the screen door.

"Hello, I'm Robert Mulligan." The tall, slender dark-haired gentleman opened the screen door and reached out his hand toward the detective.

"I'm Detective Chavez. I'd like to speak with you about your mother's death." He reciprocated to the offered handshake.

"Come in," Robert said as he opened the door for the detective. "You are welcome to have a seat in the front room." He pointed to the room directly behind him, which contained a huge flat-screen television and two light-brown couches. "Can I get you some water or something to drink?"

Detective Chavez noted that the room was located in the back of the house and was clearly not the "front room" as described by Robert; however, it gave him a chance to view both sides of the home, so the detective ignored the faux pas and proceeded to the couch that faced the front door, handing his card to Robert as he went past him.

"No, thank you," he responded and settled in. He waited for Robert to get comfortable before continuing. "First, Mr. Mulligan, please allow me to express my condolences for your loss."

"Thank you."

"I just have a few routine questions to ask you."

"Okay, that's fine."

"Mr. Mulligan, where do you work?"

"I own a couple of gas stations, but right now, I'm spending most of my time at the newest station."

"Could you tell me where you were last Monday, in the early morning hours?"

"I was at work."

"What time do you go to work?"

"I normally leave the house at five a.m."

"Did anyone see you leave at that time?"

"Yes, my wife. She fixed my lunch, prepared some coffee, and saw me off. Most everyone else in the neighborhood isn't out and about until much later in the morning."

"Do you punch a time clock at work, Mr. Mulligan?"

"No. I own the business, but my assistant manager could verify what time I arrived."

"What is your assistant manager's name?"

"Ted Wagner."

"Do you have an address and/or phone number for Mr. Wagner?" The detective pulled out his notepad and Montblanc black pen and waited for the information.

"I have his address in my personnel files, but they're at work. His phone number is 321-207-2853."

Detective Chavez jotted down the number. "Mr. Mulligan, how long does it take you to drive to work?"

"About thirty minutes, depending on traffic, of course."

"And were you there all day?"

"Yes, and you can verify that as well."

"Mr. Mulligan, when did you last speak with your mother?"

"I usually see her on Wednesdays. So that would have been the last time I saw her or spoke to her."

"Can you tell me about that visit? Was there anything out of the ordinary that you might have noticed?"

"No. It was the same as usual. It had become difficult to have a normal conversation with her. She would comprehend a sentence here and there, but her answers were usually sort of off-the-wall. I'm sure her responses weren't what she meant to say, but she had little control over how she responded. She was just so very confused all the time."

"I understand that you and your siblings were getting ready to put your mother into a nursing home. Is that correct?"

He laughed. "Yes, we talked about it, but we never got much further than that. Every time we talked, we'd fight about something or another." Robert fidgeted in his seat.

"What would you and your siblings fight about?"

Detective Chavez watched Robert rub his arm with the palm of his left hand several times then scratch with his fingertips. He wondered if Robert was nervous about the question.

"We'd fight about a lot of things."

"Can you give me some examples?"

"Yes. About the nursing home—no one could decide on a specific one. Meanwhile, my mother would continue to burn holes in the furniture and her clothing with her cigarettes." He paused. "Then there was always the issue of money."

"Like what issues of money?" he interrupted.

"Carrie thinks everyone was misusing our mother's money. She would accuse everyone of one thing or another." Robert rubbed the back of his neck as he spoke.

"Did she accuse you of anything?"

"Yes. She accused everyone."

"What did she accuse you of?"

"She thought I was using our mom's money to pay for the gardener to mow my lawn as well as my mom's yard."

"And is there any truth to that?"

"Well"—he paused and rubbed his neck again and lowered his voice—"that only happened once." Robert twisted his head on his neck, and the bones let off a cracking sound that could be heard quite clearly across the room.

"And anything else? Any issues with the other siblings?"

"Yes, but you should probably talk to my sisters about that."

"I understand there was an issue about Carrie bringing in a conservator. How did you feel about that?"

"I didn't agree. We didn't need any outsiders in this. It's a family matter. Carrie just got carried away with this law-school thing of hers."

Detective Chavez could see that Robert held some anger or resentment about this issue.

"Mr. Mulligan, do you know of anyone who would want to hurt your mother?"

"No. Her illness has been really hard on all of us, but I don't think any of us would want to hurt her or kill her." He shifted his body in his seat to turn sideways, bending one leg onto the sofa where he sat.

"How has the illness been hard on you, Mr. Mulligan?"

"We all—well, almost all of us, felt obligated to help in the care of our mother. But none of us really had any qualifications to care for an elderly woman with Alzheimer's. I mean none of us has any healthcare knowledge of any kind. In fact, none of us even knew what Alzheimer's was before Mom was diagnosed with it."

"You said, "Almost all of us felt obligated. What did you mean by that?"

"Well, it seems that Colleen couldn't be bothered to come see Mom, just too busy living her own life, and Mary Ann pulled away from the family years ago."

"You also used the word 'obligated' to care for your mother. Did you feel that your mother's illness was a burden?"

"Well, yes. It was a burden to everyone. It was really hard on those of us that made any effort at all." He paused and straightened his position on the couch. "We all have families and lots of obligations to handle, and then when Dad died suddenly, we all got slammed by a new and added burden." He lowered his voice. "And now everyone is fighting. We never fought before that. The family has really fallen apart over the last couple of years."

Detective Chavez made no comment and waited for Robert to continue after a brief period of silence.

"It's like we lost our mother too, shortly after Shawn died. She just wasn't mentally present in her body anymore—maybe even before he died. He used to say she was sick but never went into detail. After a while, I don't think any of us knew who we were talking to anymore. She was a stranger to everyone, including herself." Robert looked down at his folded hands that lay in his lap.

"I understand it's a difficult disease for families to deal with." Detective Chavez empathized.

"Yes, it is. It just isn't fair to anyone who has to be involved. The entire family becomes the victim of the disease."

"Did it make you want to put an end to it for your mother's sake?"

Robert raised his head and his voice. "Detective, are you asking me if I killed my mother? Because if that's what you're getting at, you're barking up the wrong tree. I would never have hurt my mother."

"Sorry to upset you, Mr. Mulligan, but it's my job to ask questions in order to find out who did kill your mother."

"Yes, I suppose it is, but I had nothing to do with it," he said sternly.

"Any idea as to who might have killed your mother?"

"No, but then that's your job to find out, right?"

"Yes." He paused while wondering why Robert's disposition had been so volatile. "Well, that should be enough for today." He paused again for a few short seconds. "Mr. Mulligan, do you take any medications?"

"I take medicine for high blood pressure, but that's all." He got up from the couch and stood, watching the detective.

Detective Chavez got up as well. He could tell Robert was inviting him to leave.

"Thank you for your time, Mr. Mulligan. I'll be in touch, but please feel free to call me if you have anything you think I should know." He walked to the door and out to his car.

He felt drained. It was taxing to interview individuals while being alert to their every move, their demeanor, and trying to figure out what truth might be hidden between the words they uttered.

He would stop by the office to check for any messages that might be waiting or reports that had been turned in while he had been out in the field, before going home for a few hours' rest and a bite to eat.

CHAPTER
TWENTY-FOUR

Carrie was anxious to get off the bus and speak to a supervisor about the phone calls she was entitled to. She knew her chances of talking to anyone would be nil if she slipped up and called this officer of the law by the nickname she had given her. She glanced at the name tag on Ms. Piggy's shirt.

"Officer Tittle, I'd like to speak to a supervisor about some calls I need to make."

"In good time, in good time. Move along now."

Carrie felt anger rise within but controlled it, knowing it would only be to her disadvantage to let it show. She dutifully walked into the facility and followed in line with the others toward the control desk. She leaned in toward the speaker that was embedded in the center of the glass window.

"Excuse me, but I need to speak with someone regarding phone calls that I should have been allowed to make."

"Yes," responded a large black officer with beautiful features. "You'll be allowed to make phone calls once we get all of you transferred to your assigned pods. You'll need to be a little patient. Officer Tittle will direct you to the assigned areas, and the officer in your pod will assist you with your needs."

"Thank you." Carrie was impatient and irritated, but she was aware that everything was out of her control here, and she had no choice but to follow instructions.

"Listen up," yelled Ms. Piggy, "you are to go back to your rooms to collect the personal-hygiene items you were given during processing and come back to this spot in two minutes!"

The heavy metal gate opened to allow the detainees into the hallway. The doors to each cell buzzed one by one, allowing the females to grab their items and return to the heavy gate that had closed behind them.

Carrie grabbed her toothpaste, toothbrush, toilet paper, and thin hand towel and shoved them into the black net carry bag that she had been given. She hurried back to the metal gate. She was anxious to get her pod assignment. She desperately needed to be able to talk to David and find out if he'd gotten an attorney for her.

Ms. Piggy came from the control room and into the open area. She instructed the officer inside the room to open the gate for the detainees to return to her for their pod assignments, which were written on the paper on her clipboard. "Ms. Martinez, pod 2. Stand over here." Ms. Piggy directed her to the left of her. "Ms. Jackkect, pod 3. Stand on this side." The officer directed her to the right of her. "Mrs. Stern, pod 4. Stay right there." Ms. Piggy continued with the remaining detainees as three female officers came out of the control room to assist with the disbursing of the detainees to their assigned pods.

Carrie and a small Asian woman were assisted by the beautiful large black officer. Her features were striking. Carrie would have guessed she was mulatto, since her lips, nose, and hair all resembled the features of a white person and her skin was a soft chocolate brown. Carrie had long ago decided that mulatto women were usually very attractive, almost as if the mulatto child had been blessed with the best characteristics each parent had to offer. Usually anyway, she thought. It was the huge size of this woman that disturbed Carrie's neat classification of this officer. One of her parents, or someone in her ancestry, must have been part giant, she thought. The woman stood six foot four, maybe more.

"I'm Officer Okeke. I'll take you to pod 4. Once you get assigned a bunk, you can request to see the pod counselor about those phone calls." She looked directly at Carrie as she spoke. "In fact, you'll get some good information from your pod counselor, if you chose to listen to it. Follow me." She headed down the hallway on the other side of the glassed-in control room.

Surprisingly, the huge metal gate was absent. They walked down several different hallways until they came to a locked glass door. Officer

Okeke spoke into the black mic on her left shoulder. A loud buzz sounded, and the officer opened the door. She led them past several hallways and then stopped at the fourth hallway, blocked by yet another glass door. She again spoke into the mic, and the door slid to one side, allowing entry.

"This is pod 4. You'll be here until formal charges are filed, and at that time, you'll be assigned your very own personal cell, which holds two inmates. This pod holds twenty-four, and the officer over at the desk in the middle will assign a bunk to each of you. Good luck, ladies."

Officer Okeke turned and went out the open door, which closed quickly behind her. Carrie and her fellow detainee stood, watching the females in the pod check them out. It was a very diverse group, thought Carrie. The officer from the desk in the center of the room approached with a clipboard in her hand.

"I'm Officer Stykes. I will be your resident officer Monday, Wednesday, and Friday. You'll meet a couple of other officers as the week progresses." She raised her clipboard, flipped the first page into the air, and read from the next page. "Stern, you will be assigned to bunk 19. Thomas, you'll be assigned to bunk 22. Put your personal items in the cubicle at the foot of your bed."

"Officer Stykes, when would I be able to see the pod counselor?"

"What do you want to see the pod counselor for?"

"I need to make some phone calls." Carrie felt self-conscious being watched and listened to by everyone in the pod.

"You don't have to see the pod counselor for that." She pointed to a pay phone on the pillar to the left side of the room. "There's a phone right there. Local calls are free. If your call requires fees, they're taken from your commissary funds. All conversations are monitored by control, so keep that in mind."

"Really, you listen to our calls," Carrie said in surprise.

"You lost your right to privacy when you entered this establishment. The only thing you can do in private now is urinate and take a dump. Everything else is communal. Meals are brought in, and you'll eat at the tables over there." She pointed to a small area that held four long tables that were attached to the floor by huge nuts and bolts. "Everyone is responsible for cleaning the pod they reside in, so you'll be getting your list of chores before the day is over. Any questions?"

Both Carrie and her fellow detainee shook their head.

"Okay, put your personal items in your cubicle, and relax. You've got nothing but time on your hands now. Keep out of trouble and keep to yourselves, and you should be fine."

"Thanks," said Carrie as she walked over to the white metal bunk, which held a rolled blue-and-white striped mattress at the end, with a folded blue blanket on top of it. The number 19 was painted in large black numbers at the end of the bed. She was pleased it was the top of the two bunks, and loved the fact that it was also in the corner with a wall on one side, allowing her a little more privacy than the bunk across from her, which had no walls at all and stood open to everything. Carrie placed her personal items in the cubicle at the end of the bed and unrolled the mattress upon the metal frame, put the blanket at the bottom, and wondered why she had no pillow. She sat on her mattress and watched her fellow inmates mill about the cafeteria-size room. She noticed several people playing board games. She watched others walk in and out of a sun filled area at the back of the pod which appeared to be utilized as a basketball court. She noticed a person dressed in black slacks and a white cook's jacket enter the pod with a six-foot tall metal cart. Suddenly, her stomach growled, and she could smell warm food. She guessed this was lunch. She waited before leaving her bunk. She wanted to make sure she understood the protocol and/or hierarchy in her new surroundings. She watched.

"Stern, if you want lunch, you'd better get over here," stated Officer Stykes. "You only get twenty minutes to consume your meal."

Carrie said nothing but came down from her perch and walked over to the trays lined up inside the metal cart. She grabbed a tray and sat at one of the few empty spots left at the tables.

She sat next to an older lady; her hair was gray and disheveled.

"Hello," said Carrie.

"Keep to yourself, honey, if you want to survive in here," the old lady spit out without looking up.

Carrie didn't respond, just nodded her understanding. She viewed the contents of the plastic-molded tray and its various compartments, but nothing looked appealing, and although her stomach growled with hunger, she suddenly didn't feel hungry at all. She picked up the sandwich and took one bite and chewed slowly while playing with the plastic spork. Two bites was all she could manage.

"Okay, it's time to clean up. Trays back in the cart. Let's go." Officer Stykes spoke loudly but seemed careful not to let her voice rise to a yell.

CHAPTER
TWENTY-FIVE

Carrie had walked around the perimeter of the pod close to a dozen times when she decided it was time to interrupt Officer Stykes, who appeared intent on her computer work. Carrie didn't want to irritate her gatekeeper. She walked up slowly and quietly stood next to the desk without uttering a sound, waiting for the officer to look in her direction.

"Yes, Stern, what is it?"

"I'd like to make a phone call, please."

"If the phone is unoccupied, help yourself." She never raised her head during the exchange of words and continued typing on the keyboard. "Five minutes, Stern."

"Yes, sir." She hurried over to the pillar that held the pay phone. She hadn't seen a pay phone in years, she thought, as she picked up the receiver and listened for a dial tone. She dialed and heard two rings before someone picked up.

"David, why weren't you at court today with an attorney?" Her voice was harsh.

"Well, hello to you too, Carrie."

"Sorry. I only have five minutes to talk, so I don't have time for niceties right now."

"The attorney I spoke to will come to the jail to talk to you. I had a tough time getting someone who didn't demand a huge retainer fee. It's not like we're swimming in money, dear."

"Yes, I know. Do you know when he'll be coming?"

"Visiting hours tomorrow, I suspect. His name is Dick Nash."

"How are the children?" Carrie's voice had softened.

"We're all fine, Carrie. You just worry about yourself right now, and I'll worry about the kids."

"Thanks, David. I'll try. Kiss the kids for me, please."

"Sure. Take care." He hung up quickly.

Carrie hesitated to hang up and end the connection to the world she loved—her children. Carrie was feeling a huge distance between herself and David, but now she also felt angry and disappointed in him. She felt very alone.

She looked around to see who had listened in on her conversation, noticed no one, and went over to her bunk. She climbed up the rungs of the ladder and lay on her mattress. She settled in as best she could on the thin, lumpy mattress and rolled the blanket she had been given to use as a pillow. She stared at the ceiling, tracing the texture of it with her eyes in an effort to ignore the sounds of the flat-screen television, which played for the few inmates that cared to watch it during the allotted two hours.

Carrie felt the tightness in her chest as her heartache increased by the feeling of betrayal by her beloved husband. He didn't seem to care that she was in jail, away from her children and her home. Caged unjustly, with people she would have avoided at all costs in her ordinary life. *What could he be thinking?* she wondered. Seconds later the answer came to her. He was thinking of his young firm-body girlfriend and not the mother of his children. It had been one thing to cheat on her with another woman. That seemed like nothing more than sex with a younger women. It might have been forgivable given the fact they had been married more than ten years, had had his children and her body wasn't as sexy as it had once been. Men were weak that way and she didn't really believe David loved the younger women. It had just been sex, nothing more. But now she needed him to been there for her, but he had failed her. *The SOB. I guess I'll need an attorney that handles criminal and divorce cases,* she thought as she turned to her side upon the thin mattress.

The hours dragged on, and her stomach growled with anger since she'd passed on dinner as well as lunch, but still she felt better than she had this morning. She felt a sense of relief after she had been able to talk to David, who had given the smallest bit of hope that she would be able to talk to an attorney soon. He was being very unsupportive and cold, but it was her only glimmer of hope that this awful mess would soon come to an end.

Carrie was feeling like a victim once again. It had started with her mother's disease, turning the lives of each member of the family upside down, but now her siblings had accused her of the death of her mother. She feared the circumstances were conspiring to take her freedom and her children from her for a very long time, maybe for the rest of her life. The tears rolled from her eyes onto the rolled up blanket. She stared at the ceiling, wondering what she had done or failed to do that made David turn his heart away from her. Why had he not been there? Why had he not made every effort to get her out of jail immediately? How could he care so little about what he was doing to the children they had created out of love they once felt for each other. Was this really what life was to hold for her? She longed to let out loud sobs in an effort to release the pain but she instinctively knew she had to hold her urges in check in this environment of tough, bitter, women who would laugh, jeer, and bully her for her female weaknesses.

She closed her eyes and laid her hands on top of her stomach. She concentrated on her breathing the way she had been taught in her meditation class. Inhale, hold, exhale. Listen to the breathing, shut all else out of your thoughts, she told herself. She had practiced many times but with little success, but now she needed to relax and shut out all external noises. It was a matter of survival. She gave her mind permission to take her away from her surroundings.

Carrie recalled that she had never liked her mother as a person. She had always known she would have never picked her out as a friend. But now she saw her mother in a different light, not because she was dead but because of the memories that kept coming back to her. She realized that Maggie had struggled to survive despite the disease that had stripped her of the person she had once been. Carrie wondered why we humans hang on to life so dearly. Was it really the fear of death, or was it the fear of what comes after death? Carrie didn't know; however, she did know that Maggie had tried valiantly to live on, even after her entire world had collapsed when her husband had suddenly died. *Poor Mom,* thought Carrie, she had been so very dependent on her husband for her existence, and then to be left all alone in a world where she had no one but her children, who were too busy living their own lives, to be there when she needed them. Life was so unfair.

Carrie recalled the morning from five months after Shawn's death when she had brought little Warner down to the kitchen and set him into his high chair for breakfast. Maggie was sitting at the table smoking a cigarette.

"Good morning, Mom."

"Is it?" Maggie replied.

"What's wrong, Mom? You sound really down."

The tears slid down Maggie's face. Carrie grabbed the box of Kleenex from the top of the refrigerator. There were boxes of tissues in every room since Maggie's arrival. She set the box in front of Maggie and proceeded to prepare some cold cereal for Warner. Maggie rested her cigarette on the edge of the ashtray and pulled several tissues from the box.

"Thank you." She wiped the tears and reached for her jeweled cigarette case. "I don't know what to do. I guess I had better go home." She lit a cigarette and puffed, while the one she had laid down only a moment ago burned in the ashtray.

"Mom, you already have cigarette lit there in the ashtray."

"Oh." She stubbed the newest one out, pushing hard enough to bend it in the middle.

"What should I do, Carrie?" The tears continued rolling down Maggie's face.

"Well, Mom, I really don't think I should make that decision for you, but I do think it's time to get on with your life. It's only been five months since Dad died, but you still have to go on living."

"Yeah, I think so too. Damn him. Why did he have to go away?" Maggie extinguished the cigarette that lay in the ashtray, which was almost burned to the filter.

"Mom, did you take your antidepressant pill last night?"

"No, I don't think so."

"The doctor said you really should take them for a while." Carrie paused. "Dad didn't go away by choice, Mom. He certainly wouldn't have put you through this on purpose."

"Then why didn't he go see a doctor when he didn't feel well?" Maggie wiped her nose with the wet tissue.

"I know, Mom. Dad's entire family was like that. They hated going to doctors. I guess they were afraid they'd never come out of the hospital once they got in. It was the Old World beliefs his parents brought from Ireland."

"Damn him," Maggie repeated.

"Mom, you're welcome to stay here as long as you like, so don't worry about it. Okay?"

Carrie remembered picking up the Cheerios that Warner pushed off the top of the high chair to the floor.

"I think I'd better go home."

"Well, think about it for a few days, Mom. You have a doctor appointment in two days, so you'd have to be here for that anyway."

Carrie's mind shifted to the time when she had taken Maggie to the doctor. Carrie remembered that she couldn't believe what her mother was experiencing was only grief. She recalled that her father had said he thought Maggie was sick, but even when asked, he never went into detail about the symptoms or reasons he felt that way. He had never been the sort of person to complain about anything so Carrie knew his concern was deep and that he was greatly troubled when he spoke of Maggie's forgetfulness and extreme dependency on him. He mentioned that Maggie had always kept the family checkbook, but now she could no longer successfully add or subtract the numbers. Carrie had been noticing the same sort of things in her mother since she had come to stay with her. Maggie couldn't function without depending on others, and Carrie was beginning to feel the strain of her mother's severe dependency. Carrie decided it was time to find out for certain.

"Hurry, Mom." Carrie remembered urging her as they crossed the busy downtown street on the day of the doctor appointment.

"I am," replied Maggie even though her pace remained snaillike.

Carrie's mind injected a memory from her childhood. She recalled when she was a little girl, she could barely catch up to her mother's fast walking pace. *Wow, how things change,* she thought.

The cars had slowed as Maggie did her best to reach the opposite side. "Sorry, Mom, we should have used the crosswalk, I guess."

"I'm all right. What's the hurry anyway?"

"We're late for the appointment."

Once upstairs Carrie sat Maggie down and let the receptionist know they were there. It was only a few minutes before a female doctor came out to greet them.

"Hello," she said, "I'm Dr. Puddan." She turned toward Carrie. "Can I speak to you first?" she said. The doctor then turned to address Maggie. "Hello, Mrs. Murphy. I'd like to speak with your daughter, and then I'll have you come into my office. We'll be right back."

"Mom, I'll be right back." Carrie had tried to reassure her mother as she left her alone in the waiting room.

"Yeah," said Maggie with a sour tone.

Carrie could tell by her mother's tone of voice that she didn't like this. Once inside the doctor's office, she took a seat.

"I understand you made this appointment for your mother."

"Yes, that's right."

"I thought it best that you explain to me what the situation is before I see your mother."

"Well, my mother has been extremely forgetful lately. She asks the same questions over and over. She can't remember what day of the week it is or the calendar date. I'm very concerned. Her husband passed away about five months ago, so it might just be grief."

"Do you feel that her forgetfulness is due to grief, or do you feel it exceeds that?"

"I don't know. That's why I brought her here. Although I told her it was to see about vitamins to make her feel better and maybe help her gain some weight. She's so awfully thin."

"There's really more to it, isn't there?" Dr. Puddan was blunt, thought Carrie, but in a gentle way.

"Yes. My father complained of these symptoms about a year before he died, so no, I don't think it's just grief. I guess I'm afraid it might be Alzheimer's disease."

"What makes you think that?"

Carrie remembered that she had thought Dr. Puddan lacked bedside manner during the conversation.

"Well, I recently spoke with a neighbor whose father died of Alzheimer's a short time ago, and the symptoms sounded a lot like what my mother is displaying.

"Okay, I'll speak with you again after I see your mother."

Dr. Puddan followed Carrie back into the waiting room.

"Mrs. Murphy, would you please come back to my office?" She held out her hand toward Maggie.

Carrie remembered that her mother was unhappy about what was taking place. She was silent, and her mouth was scrunched up, making her look mad; nevertheless, Maggie reluctantly followed the doctor.

Twenty minutes or so passed before Maggie and the doctor came back to the waiting room.

"Can I speak with you once more?" she said to Carrie.

"What am I, a child?" said Maggie under her breath as she sat down.

Carrie ignored the remark and followed Dr. Puddan to her office.

"I've dealt with a lot of Alzheimer's patients in the past, and I feel sure that your mother has the disease." She paused. "In order for you and your family to fully understand what you're dealing with, I suggest you pick up the book *The 36-Hour Day* by Nancy Mace and Peter Rabins. It'll prepare you for what you're about to face."

"Aren't there tests she could take or something, to be sure?

"I think you should take her for a complete physical so we can eliminate any doubts your family may have. That's all we can do with Alzheimer's. We can only simply eliminate any other causes of the dementia."

"Okay."

"I'll set up an appointment for her and give you a call with the date. Is any one day better than the other?"

"No. I'll make sure she gets here."

While the doctor typed on her computer keyboard, Carrie looked down the long, narrow room and noticed a dollhouse and several children's toys she had not noticed on the first visit to the office.

Dr. Puddan's attention returned to Carrie. "I'm 90 percent sure that what your mother has is Alzheimer's. I asked her a few questions, and she couldn't tell me who the president of the United States was or what month it was. She also got very irritated and stated she didn't read the paper anymore. However, these are very simple questions that most anyone should be able to answer. We'll do all the routine tests just to make sure. I've submitted a request for a total physical examine. We'll call you when a date has been assigned."

"Thank you, Doctor. I'll pick up several books and give them to my brother and sisters. None of them thinks it's as bad as I do, but then they don't have her living with them either. Can my brother or sisters call you if they don't believe me?"

Carrie remembered Dr. Puddan's smile at the last remark.

"Yes, anytime." She reached into her desk drawer and pulled out several business cards and handed them to Carrie.

"Thank you."

Carrie remembered leaving the doctor's office knowing that her life would never be the same. She also remembered her mother's angry glance when she got back to the waiting room.

"Why did she ask me such stupid questions? What are you trying to do to me?"

"Mom, I'm only trying to help. I want you to feel better." She paused. "The doctor wants you to have a physical. They'll check your blood and urine to see if vitamins will help you. I hate seeing you so depressed all the time, and you're so very thin."

"You just want them to put me away. My husband dies, and my kids try to have me committed." Her voice rose, and tears began to fall down her cheeks.

"Mom, that's not true. I love you. I wouldn't let anyone put you away." Carrie recalled the silence between the two of them that existed during the remainder of the trip home. It would be impossible for her to explain to her mother what was truly going on and how the disease she had would affect her life.

The memories were painful but provided an escape from the reality of being in jail.

"Lights-out in fifteen!" yelled Officer Stykes.

Carrie got down from her bunk, grabbed her toothbrush and toothpaste, and waited in line to use the restroom. She only hoped she'd reach it before the inmates were ordered to stand for roll call and then ordered to turn off the lights and retire for the evening.

CHAPTER
TWENTY-SIX

Carrie lay as still as she could even though the urge to toss and turn was great. The bed was narrow and didn't provide much room to move around. She didn't want to make a lot of noise and disturb the others, since she was not yet sure who was friend and who was foe in her new environment, and had no desire to find out who was foe.

Carrie stared at the ceiling and allowed her mind to take her to a time when her brother and sister had actually worked together in an effort to help their mother. That was all gone now.

Once the family had learned that Maggie did indeed have Alzheimer's disease, they had decided to allow Maggie to go back home to Newcastle in one last ditch attempt to allow her to retain some shed of independence and dignity. It didn't last long.

Carrie remembered how her mother would keep calling and ask if she could come visit. She said she was lonely and the neighbors didn't seem to pay any attention to her. Carrie understood what the neighbors must be feeling. It was difficult to be around Maggie now, even for the family. Maggie had told Carrie that she would wake up thinking someone was in bed with her, and then she'd lie awake all night listening for the sound of the garage door to open and listen for Shawn's car pulling in after a day at work. But it didn't happen anymore; he was gone, never to come home again.

When Maggie attempted to drive down to see Carrie, it took four hours instead of the one hour it should have taken. Somehow, somewhere along the way, she vanished in time, or so it seemed. No one knew where she had gotten lost or where she had ended up when she finally realized that she was not where she was supposed to be. The good news was that eventually she came back to reality and would, somehow, find her way to Carrie's house. Carrie recalled that this was a real feat for Maggie since she had never been responsible for driving when Shawn was alive; she was always the passenger. Carrie understood that Maggie was trying so very hard to be independent and exist without her lifelong partner.

Maggie got lost driving to Carrie's house twice before the family got together and decided a change had to take place. They all agreed that maybe next time Maggie got lost, she wouldn't be able to find that lucid moment that in the past allowed her to find her way home. It was scary for everyone.

They also agreed it was time for Maggie to be moved closer to her children. They would start packing the following weekend and then paint the interior of Maggie's home the weekend after. Every room in the entire house had the yellowish-brown smoke grime on the walls from Maggie's chain-smoking.

Carrie recalled that the move went quickly. Carrie and Bill had driven up early with the truck Bill had rented the evening before. Helen and Maggie were to follow after they had gotten the keys to the town house Maggie was going to rent. Robert and Kathy had assured everyone that they would be up early but had arrived several hours late. Helen had commented that it must have been a tennis game that kept them, since Kathy arrived with her short tennis outfit on.

Carrie, Helen, and Kathy packed quickly, while Bill and Robert loaded the boxes into the rented truck. Maggie tried to help pack, but of course, she'd forgotten how. She still attempted to go through the motions but accomplished little.

Carrie remembered with fondness that David had offered to stay home with the children so she could do what she felt she needed to do for her mother. She knew that much more would get done this way since she was far more physical than David. She always liked the fact that he was the more intelligent one, although she seldom listened to his advice. He was extremely smart but lacked common sense. Besides, both she and Colleen had inherited their father's stubbornness and none of their mother's dependency.

Carrie recalled that the family had made several trips back and forth with Maggie's treasures. Bill unilaterally decided that Helen had done enough packing and lifting, so he announced to everyone that she would drive down with him and she would stay at the town house to unpack items. After they left for the town house, Robert decided that he would go get a bucket of chicken for dinner. Since the kitchen floor was strewn with newsprint for wrapping, the four of them spread out a blanket on the front room floor and pretended to be having a picnic. It was good psychological therapy for the weary movers. She remembered thinking how it was amazing that during a move, the kitchen always turned out to be a bigger job than planned. It was good to have the help of her siblings.

Maggie was getting tired and irritable, so it was decided that they would quit for the day and start again tomorrow. The next day came all too soon. All the siblings complained of sore muscles, but it was common knowledge that the work had to be finished if the painting of the interior were to happen the following weekend.

Carrie reminisced about the feeling of cooperation and love between siblings during the time of moving her mother. In fact, she recalled Robert mentioning his feelings regarding that very emotion. She recalled she had driven her station wagon that Sunday, with Robert and Kathy as passengers, in order to finish packing that weekend when Robert had brought up the subject. "You know, since Dad passed away, it really makes you start appreciating the people around you."

"Yeah, it sort of jolts you into awareness," Carrie remembered replying.

Robert continued. "I called my father last week and told him we never spend much time together and we should get together to play golf."

"Oh, don't you see him much?" She had always been under the impression that he saw his real father quite often.

"No, I haven't seen much of him in the past year or so. Everyone just gets too busy living their lives."

Carrie felt as if she were again present in the past. She felt her chest and throat tighten. She recalled her alter ego telling her that he still had a father but she didn't. She began to feel how unfair it was that her father was gone, and although Robert and Helen professed that Shawn was their dad, she started feeling resentment toward them. One of the most important persons in her life had been snatched away from her unexpectedly in a matter of minutes, and although she had thought it was a heartache that they had all shared together, she now realized her heartache was deeper and more devastating to her than it probably had been to them. Robert now had a second chance to make his relationship with his biological father more meaningful. She didn't, and although she had always done her best to let her father know he was loved, she felt cheated—cheated out of future times she wished to share with him and talks she wished to have, lots of moments that would never happen now.

As she remembered the pain of loss and the tears that accompanied the hurt, her tears formed in the corner of her eyes and began to roll down the sides of her face onto the dirty mattress.

Carrie remembered the many times Robert had caused chaos in the household during his rebellious teenage years, always yelling that he didn't have to listen to her father and yelling that he wasn't his real father. Yes, she now realized how the resentment and distance between the siblings had grown and festered.

Carrie turned slowly and carefully to her side. She didn't want to wake anyone in the pod and create a situation she really didn't want to be confronted with. She wiped the tears from her face with the back of her hand. She wished her memories would go away and her mind would occupy itself with something else, but the memories continued involuntarily.

Her mind took her back into the car again, driving to Newcastle for the last of her mother's treasures. She remembered trying to push the negative feelings from her heart and mind, but the bitterness had begun. She changed the subject regarding their father. "It's too bad Bill's been out of work for so long. What's he going to do?" She waited for either Robert or Kathy to respond.

"I guess he's looking. His severance pay is almost gone though." Kathy had always had a close relationship with Helen and gotten a lot of insider information from her.

"He's such a know-it-all." Carrie stopped short, knowing this was a negative comment, and she had made an effort to stop the negativity.

Robert picked the comment up. "Yeah, well, he'll come up with something. He did the last two times he lost his job."

"I hope so. Helen was planning on quitting two months ago but can't until Bill goes back to work," Kathy said.

More insider information, thought Carrie.

The three talked about general issues the rest of the way to Newcastle. Carrie recalled they had gotten everything out of the house that day and decided to deal with the patio furniture the following weekend when they would return to paint the interior of the house in order for it to be put up for sale that same week.

Carrie's mind jumped forward to the painting of the interior of the house, when Robert and Kathy showed up hours past the agreed start time. However, the siblings were still getting along at that point, she thought. Then she recalled the money. It was the second move of her mother that started the devastation of her family, she thought. Her mind stopped to inspect with hindsight what had occurred.

She had felt pleased with herself when she had fought the landlady of the town house to get the deposit her mother had placed for the rental, and won. Carrie had done some research and pulled and copied cases to present to the landlady, proving that the landlady's refusal to return the deposit of a terminally ill person was unconscionable. Carrie had won, and the deposit had been returned to Maggie.

No one was thrilled to be moving Maggie a second time, but she had been very unhappy in the small town-house that had been too small to house all of Maggie's treasures. Most of them remained packed and stored in the one car garage that came with the rental. Maggie had complained relentlessly. It was only when Carrie's close friend purchased a new two-bedroom home with full dining room that the kids had agreed to move her once more so she could unpack the greatest portion of her belongings and display them in her several china and curio cabinets.

Carrie remembered going into the rental to survey the situation and was pleasantly surprised when she was confronted by many packed boxes standing ready for the move. Maggie had packed all week in happy anticipation of the move. Carrie had felt such pity for her mother, but every now and then, she would be amazed how hard Maggie tried to hide the fact that she was ill. She didn't know when her mother was lucid or when she was confused and unaware of the reality of her world. One minute she seemed normal, and the next she was a different person. It was evident that this disease took more than just one victim. Its reach scratched, bit, and scarred everyone in the family. Every one of them were victims.

Carrie recalled that it felt as if her mother died a little every day, almost as if the person she had known had almost totally disappeared, and only tiny remnants remained in the shell of what once was her mother.

Carrie recalled the details of the day of the second move as she lay quietly and restlessly on her bed.

"Good morning, Mom." Carrie had kissed her cheek. "Are you excited about the move?"

"Yes. It'll be so nice to have room to put out all my treasures."

Robert, Kathy, Helen, and Bill were there as well. All working together, thought Carrie. But that was the day. *Well, there really wasn't just one day,* she thought. There were many days that created the spiral of destruction within their family.

It had been near noon when most of the packing was done and boxes were in short supply. Helen had suggested that she and Maggie go to the new house and unpack some of the boxes that had been delivered by the fellows. That way, the emptied boxes could be used again for the remaining items. Besides, she'd pick up something for lunch and would have it ready when the next truck load was delivered. Everyone agreed that the idea was a good one, especially since Helen's back was hurting her and unpacking the boxes would be easier for her than moving the boxes from the town house to the truck.

Carrie had completed the front room and moved to her mother's bedroom while Robert and Bill loaded the boxes from the garage, which had never been unpacked during Maggie's nine-month stay at the town-house rental. Kathy had gone to a moving company to purchase more boxes. It had seemed there was no end to the amount of personal property Maggie owned, and it all had to be moved, or Maggie would surely miss the smallest of items, even though she couldn't remember what happened yesterday.

Carrie recalled sitting on the closet floor tossing socks, slippers, nylons, and miscellany into a bag since the additional boxes had not yet arrived when she noticed a white envelope tucked underneath a throw rug. When she picked up the envelope, it seemed heavy, so instead of instinctively throwing it into the bag, she opened it to investigate. *Wow*, she had thought, as she shuffled through a stack of one-hundred-dollar bills. She had been surprised, but as she thought about it, she guessed her mother's brother, who was very wealthy, had given it to her. He had been very generous to everyone over the years. Carrie remembered getting up to go find someone to share the find with. She ran into Robert first. She flashed the wad of cash in front of him. "I found this at the bottom of Mom's closet. I'll bet Mom got this money from her brother the last time she saw him."

"How much is there?"

"I don't know. I didn't stop to count it."

He took the envelope that Carrie had held out and removed the cash from the envelope. He counted it silently.

"Twenty-six hundred dollars." He placed the money back into the envelope.

"I think we should just deposit it in her account," said Carrie as she retrieved the full envelope. "If she's misplaced and forgotten about this much money, I don't think we should give it back to her. She'll just leave it lying around again. She probably doesn't understand the concept of cash anymore."

"Yeah, that's fine," replied Robert and returned to his task.

Carrie placed the envelope in the inside pocket of her large purse and went back to work in the bedroom.

She recalled it was late afternoon when the last of the items were loaded. It was agreed that everyone would go to the new house to unpack the boxes they had just packed and moved.

When she arrived at the new home, she approached Helen and pulled the envelope from her purse. "Helen, I found this on the floor of Mom's closet. I think we should deposit it to her account rather than let Mom misplace it again."

Helen's eyes seemed to twinkle when she opened the envelope. "I'll take care of it," she said as she slipped it into her sweater pocket.

Carrie recalled it was at that moment she felt that something had just gone awry, but said nothing. She reassured herself that Helen was handling the accounts now, since she was the oldest and the executrix of the will. It was a position of trust, so Carrie decided to trust her even though she felt odd about Helen's response after seeing the stack of hundred-dollar bills.

The siblings had unpacked everything they could possibly fit into the new, bigger residence, but still there remained unpacked boxes of treasures. It had been decided that they would build a storage area in the rafters of the garage. It was a way to get the boxes out of the sight and mind of their mother. It was an effort to keep her happy and to keep the siblings from hearing constant complaints. It had seemed to work.

CHAPTER
TWENTY-SEVEN

Carrie had fallen asleep in the early morning hours, before the sun had risen. She was awakened by what sounded like a recess bell. It was six o'clock. A voice over the speaker stated that all inmates were to stand at the foot of their beds for roll call. As Carrie got into position, she noticed the food cart being brought into the pod and pushed to the table area of the room. She rubbed her eyes and noticed that her head ached from lack of sleep, and her empty stomach hurt from refusing the food that had been provided previously.

Once Carrie had finished her scrambled eggs, toast, and sausage patty, she got up to put her molded food tray back into the food cart, when an unfamiliar officer walked up to her.

"Stern, a Mr. Nash is here to talk to you. If you go to the door, I'll buzz you out. Mr. Nash will be in the room to your right just inside the hallway and between the two security doors." Carrie quickly walked to the door and waited for the buzz that would signal an unlocked door. She went directly to the room as instructed and saw an older gray-haired gentleman in a navy pinstripe suit with light-blue shirt and dark-gray tie, sitting at a table and jotting notes.

"Hello," she said as she rounded the corner.

"Hello, Mrs. Stern, I'm Richard Nash, the attorney your husband hired. Most people just call me Dick. I'd shake your hand, but I was instructed that there was to be no contact."

"Sure, that's fine. I understand."

"Let's talk about your case. It's a serious charge."

"I didn't do it."

"I don't care if you did or didn't do it, Mrs. Stern. My job is simply to show reasonable doubt should you go to trial. I'll be getting copies of all the police records and the statements you may have made up to this point in time."

"I agreed to take a polygraph. Is that okay?"

"Sure. If you have nothing to hide, go ahead and take one. It isn't admissible in court anyway."

"Oh, okay. Then what's the purpose of it?"

"It's just an investigative tool. If you don't pass it, they'll be on top of you like butter on bread, with tons of questions. If you pass it, they simply ignore it. That's pretty much it. Are you sure you want to do that?"

"Mr. Nash, I didn't kill my mother. I have nothing to hide." Carrie's voice was strong.

"Okay. I'll do some work on your case and see if we can get you out of here. If not, the next step is the preliminary hearing. I'll be ready for it."

"Don't you have any questions for me?"

"Not yet. I have some homework to do, and then I'll be back with lots of questions. I'd appreciate it if you can sign this retainer agreement for me." He placed a two-page document in front of her. "I've brought a copy for you."

Carrie pulled the document over to her side of the table and picked up the pen that sat on top of it. "You want me to sign a document without reading it?"

"Well, Mrs. Stern, let's be honest with one another, you are in a bit of a bind, and I'm willing to take a smaller retainer than any other defense attorney would. Your husband explained your financial situation, so yes, I do suggest you sign it. You can read the copy in your spare time. I understand you have a lot of that right now."

He had a point. She needed an attorney and didn't have any money for one. She signed it and sled it back in his direction. She picked up her copy. "Thank you, Mr. Nash. I feel better now that I have an attorney to look out for my interests."

"Sure. Nice to meet you, Mrs. Stern. My phone number is on the retainer agreement."

Carrie got up from the table and walked back to the locked sliding door. The officer saw her standing there and buzzed her back into the pod. She waved her over to the control area in the center back of the pod.

"Yes?"

"Stern, you won't be assigned to a job here in the pod. At least, not until we know you're here to stay for a while. Just stay out of the way of the other inmates that have jobs to do."

"Yes, I will."

Carrie went back to her bunk, tossed the paperwork in her cubicle, and climbed to her bed in the hope she could squeak out an hour or so of sleep that she hadn't gotten last night. She lay on her back, closed her eyes, and hoped her mind and body were going to cooperate.

Her mind took her back to Helen. She remembered gently confronting Helen at the pharmacy where she had worked for almost twenty-one years. She remembered walking up to Helen at the counter.

"Hi, how are you feeling?" Carrie had carefully started the conversation.

"I'm all right." Although her voice was cheerful her eyes spoke contrarily. She looked tired.

"You look tired. Are you sure you're doing okay?"

"I'll be fine. The chiropractor told me I couldn't sleep on the waterbed anymore, and I've had trouble getting used to sleeping on the couch."

Carrie had been concerned and made many offers to help where she could, but Helen had refused all offers of help.

"I talked to Colleen the other night. I called her to tell her Mom was moved and you had hurt your back. She said she was going to call you."

"Isn't she still mad at all of us?" Helen had paused as a customer approached to pay for several items. Helen rang them up while Carrie stood back a few steps waiting for more semiprivacy. She shifted uncomfortably, wondering how to bring up the touchy subject of the money. The customer left.

"Yes, Colleen is still mad and was extremely cold during the conversation. She didn't once ask how Mom was."

"Is she really that angry that none of us have made it down to see her and Mark's new house?"

"Well, she won't have it much longer. She's letting Mark have the house when the divorce goes through. She's looking for a new one to buy."

"She must be doing well."

"No, actually she thinks she can get a good bargain on a new home since she works for a new home builder." Carrie had stepped aside for another customer buying hair-care items.

Carrie glanced at her watch and realized it was close to five and Helen would soon be off. They could talk outside, she decided.

"I'll wait for you outside," she turned and headed through the store toward the automatic door. She paced outside, wondering how to bring up the subject. It seemed so unfair to question Helen about the money when she felt so poorly. She'd try to do it gently, she thought, as she noticed Helen coming out of the building.

"Where are all the kids?"

"David's mother is down visiting for a couple of days. She's watching them."

"Helen, the bank called today. They're having trouble transferring Dad's pension, which is supposed to be deposited automatically to the new bank branch. I thought that since you set it up, you could check on it for Mom. Oh, and they don't have any record of the twenty-six hundred you deposited. Did you keep the receipt?"

Helen's eyes suddenly opened wide and appeared attentive. "Oh, I haven't had a chance to deposit it. I'll get to it Monday."

Carrie remembered feeling once again that trouble was in the air. She had wished that if Helen needed the money that badly, she would just talk to her siblings about it.

"Has Bill found a job yet?"

"No." Helen replied while reaching in her purse for car keys and headed toward her car. "He had a good offer two days ago, but we decided we didn't want to live in Florida, so he turned it down."

"Yeah, that's a long way to go for a job."

"Well, I have to get home. I'll talk to you later," said Helen as she entered her car.

Carrie remembered that she stood watching as Helen pulled away. She had hoped that what Helen said about the money was indeed true and that she wouldn't have to confront her again in the future.

But her hopes did not come to pass. She recalled that a month had gone by and the money still had not been deposited in her mother's account. Carrie remembered feeling that she was being sneaky when she had called the bank to check on the deposit, but still she felt obligated to watch out for her mother, since her father was no longer around to do so.

She dialed Robert's number.

"Hi, Robert. There's a couple of things we need to talk about." She had said and continued without hesitation. "First, the money I found in Mom's closet and gave to Helen has never been deposited into Mom's account."

Silence. Carrie could sense that Robert really didn't want to go into this.

"Robert, I'm not calling her a thief. I just think she should talk to us about it. I'm well aware Bill has been out of work for an awfully long time, but if things are that bad, why doesn't Helen turn to her family instead of pretending we won't notice that the money isn't in the account?"

"Geez, Carrie, I don't know. Just give it a little more time." Robert always had a way of talking himself out of a fight. He had been in a few scraps when he was a teenager but always seemed to get the worst end of the fight, thereby learning to avoid fighting altogether.

"What else?" His impatient voiced questioned.

"Colleen called yesterday and asked me to mention to you and Helen that she was hoping to borrow twenty thousand dollars from Mom to put down on a house."

"Yeah, I know about that. She called at seven this morning. I guess it's something we had better discuss."

Carrie could tell by his voice and his delayed reply that Robert was tired. He recently had opened another gas station, and she was aware that the new stations always posed problems in the beginning.

"How about we all get together here tomorrow evening?"

"Okay. I can come over after I feed David and the kids. Is seven okay?"

"Sure, I'll let Helen know."

Carrie recalled that when she hung up, she felt more distant from her siblings each time she spoke to any of them. She remembered envying Mary Ann and the distance she had put between her and the entire family. How nice it would be to not have to deal with any of this.

It was useless to try to sleep in this place, she thought. Her mind would not let her rest under these circumstances. Her brain had so many horrific recent events to churn through: the arrest, jail, David leaving her, the children, the attorney, and Mom's death. It was overwhelming.

CHAPTER
TWENTY-EIGHT

It was lunchtime again. The officer's voice announced roll call, and all the inmates lined up near their bunks to be counted. The lunch cart was wheeled in. The routine was becoming familiar, thought Carrie. It was a scary thought. She didn't want to get familiar with the routine of this place; she just wanted out.

The count was done, lunch was served, and she returned her food tray as usual. She ate little but felt that her body required no nourishment, since it was doing nothing physical. She had nothing to do but think of the past, the horrific present, and wonder what the future would hold. *So my mind is working overtime while my body is taking time off,* she thought as she walked toward her bunk.

The officer on duty approached her before she reached her bunk.

"Stern."

"Yes." She stopped and turned to face the officer.

"The DA's office has arranged for your polygraph test, if you're still willing to take it."

"Yes, I am."

"There's a deputy that will come to lead you to the office where the tests are administered. I'll schedule you for exercise in the yard for late this afternoon. You should be done by then."

"Thank you, I'd appreciate that."

The officer walked back to her desk, and Carrie returned to her bunk.

It was only fifteen minutes before she was instructed to follow a deputy that had entered the pod. She was taken into the elevator that was manually instructed to stop on the seventh floor. She followed the deputy a short distance to a small semidark room. She was introduced to the female polygraph examiner, Amy Newhouse. Amy then described the process while attaching sensor strips to several of Carrie's fingers. She then put a strip around her chest and a strap around her upper arm, much like a blood pressure cuff, all of which would record several physiological indices such as blood pressure, pulse, respiration, and perspiration, she explained.

Carrie made an effort to remain calm. She knew this test involved the interpretation of the fight or flight response in each person. Carrie had known for a long time now that her personality was the type that fought when she felt cornered and that she didn't run from any threat. She hoped her nervousness wouldn't cause a negative reading from the machine.

The polygraph examiner started with easy control questions and then moved on to questions that involved the case of her murdered mother. Carrie was really nervous and hoped that her truthful answers indeed registered as truthful.

She was well aware that a polygraph test was not considered reliable and, therefore, not admissible in court. She wondered if that was because the person taking the test was so darn nervous when put through this exercise that their guilt or innocence wasn't what was actually being detected. She felt her body get warm and willed herself to settle down and be calm.

It took almost three hours, and Carrie was exhausted when she was done. She was escorted back to the pod and informed by the officer that she had missed her assigned exercise time. The inmates that had been allowed to leave the pod for their assigned jobs were coming back in. It was a sign that roll call and dinner would occur next.

Carrie longed to go to her thin uncomfortable mattress, to close her eyes, and to sleep deeply for eight hours or longer. But that would have to wait until she followed the mandated routines: dinner, cleanup, and roll call before lights-out. It couldn't come fast enough, thought Carrie. She hadn't slept much at all the night before and hoped to fall asleep the minute her head hit the pillow she had acquired this afternoon.

Lights-out had finally arrived. She climbed up the ladder to her bunk, stretched out, and spread the light wool blanket over the top of her lower half. She practiced her breathing in an effort to erase the events of the day. She felt herself drifting into sleep and began to dream. She woke to the sound of her bunkmate below snoring loudly. She tossed and turned while the snoring continued. She tossed to and fro with more effort now, hoping that the shaking of the bed would wake her neighbor enough to cease the loud snoring. It worked. Carrie lay there willing her body to go back to sleep, but it refused. Her mind started up again and dragged her into thoughts from the past events concerning her siblings.

Carrie remembered walking into Robert's family room for the family meeting. She inwardly instructed her alter ego to keep her assertive nature in check. She didn't want to offend anyone and start the meeting with anger and hostility flying about, but the incident of the twenty-six hundred dollars was eating away at her. She was aware of the fact that her father had worked the swing shift for four years in order to earn a higher percentage for his pension. He had told her he wanted to provide for Maggie as well as he could if anything happened to him and she was left to fend for herself. He had worked the three to eleven shift even though Maggie constantly complained that he wasn't home with her in the evening. In fact, Carrie recalled he'd also given up many other things he had loved to do, like hunting with his brother, playing golf with his friends, spending Sunday dinner with his mother, brother, and his family, and he did so all because Maggie constantly complained. No wonder she hadn't liked her mother much, she thought.

She remembered her sister-in-law, Kathy, calling to her to bring her out of her thoughts during the family meeting. "Carrie, Carrie, earth to Carrie."

"Oh, sorry," Carrie had apologized.

"Can I get you a soft drink?"

"Yes, thank you. Whatever you have on hand is fine." Carrie turned her attention to her siblings. "Sorry, David couldn't make it. He's watching the kids."

Robert made an effort to open the meeting. "I guess the first thing we should discuss is what should be done with Mom's finances."

"Well, first of all," Bill interrupted before Robert had a chance to say more, "I've gathered a little information I think is important, and I'd like to make it known to all of you." He picked up a yellow legal pad, which had been sitting on the floor next to the brown leather recliner he sat in. He explained the figures he had gathered regarding the costs of several nursing homes and in-home care. He stated that he'd asked all the pertinent questions like how long the waiting list was, what it cost, what care was given, what liberties were allowed, who cared for the patients, among other trivial issues. He went on for fifteen to twenty minutes before stopping to take a breath or let anyone else speak.

"I don't see what you're getting at?" Carrie said.

"I'm getting at the fact that nursing homes are extremely expensive, and who knows how long Maggie will need to be in one? And you'd better consider all this when you talk finances."

"I'm sure when the time comes, we'll need that information, but I'm not sure we need it just yet." Carrie tried to sound timid.

"You know, Carrie," Bill stared at her with a long, hard glare, "we've never seen eye to eye, and we probably never will."

Carrie recalled feeling the hostility and anger bore through her. She had no idea where this hostility had started, but knew, without mistake, that it was directed toward her and only her.

Helen shifted uneasily in the plush brown velour couch as Bill continued.

"Helen and I have been to several Alzheimer's support-group meetings, and at every meeting, people tell us to distribute any and all assets of the patient two years before they have to go into a convalescent hospital."

Kathy cleared her throat before speaking. "I thought we decided not to do that. We talked about that before, Bill."

"I wasn't aware any final decision had been made, my dear," he replied.

"No final decision was made," Robert responded in an apparent effort to settle Bill down.

Carrie knew Bill behaved like this whenever he'd had a few drinks.

Robert continued. "I guess we should start making some decisions though. I've been to a support group as well, where there was a speaker from Medicare, and he made it very clear that distributing the assets of the patient in that manner was against the law."

"That may be true," Carrie said, "but Bill's right, they do keep telling families to distribute the money beforehand. Although, I'm not sure who or what we're protecting by doing that, Mom's money or our inheritance. I think we need to get more information about it before we do anything."

"Yeah, I agree," added Helen.

Bill spoke loudly, "Well, go ahead and look into it if it'll make you feel better, but I feel I know enough and have made my decision on the matter." The room became silent for a moment, and only the sound of ice cubes hitting the sides of the glass filled the strained air as Bill jostled his bourbon and seven. "Is this going to be by democratic vote?" he asked sarcastically.

"Sure. I'm just expressing my opinion. Of course, everyone's entitled to their own," replied Robert.

Carrie tried to change the subject. "Was anyone aware of the fact that Colleen was up here last week and stayed with Mom for a night?"

"Did Mom tell you that?" asked Helen as she set her soda down on the table.

"She mentioned that she'd had company. The comment was sort of a slip. She said Colleen was very upset about the divorce and that she had used up all her Kleenex."

"Yeah, Mom mentioned it to me too," Robert added.

Carrie directed her question to Robert. "Did she mention the money Colleen wants to borrow from her?"

"Yes. Mom mentioned she told Colleen she could borrow it. She kept telling me how awful Mark was treating Colleen. I guess he's not being very reasonable."

"Well, as I understand it, that's not entirely true. Colleen told me that she doesn't want to go to court and fight it out with Mark. He's offering her twenty thousand dollars for her interest in the house."

"Isn't their house worth a great deal more than that?" Bill asked.

"I think so, but they owe Mark's mother a lot of money. She advanced them the money to build it. Besides, they have a ton of bills to pay. But Mark is willing to assume those. He's also giving Colleen the newer car." Carrie shared what she had learned from Colleen directly.

Robert spoke up. "The real question here is money. Colleen wants to borrow twenty thousand dollars to purchase a home of her own. Since she's in the real estate business, she feels she can get a good deal on one of the new homes she sells for the builder."

"I think if she needs it, she should have it," said Bill as he finished off his second drink.

Kathy watched everyone intently from the entrance of the kitchen. "Would you like another Bill?"

Carrie could tell by the smile on her face she probably wanted to say "Another drinky-poo, Billy?" She and Carrie had discussed and laughed about Bill's constant drinking many times, so knowing what she was thinking was easy.

Carrie recognized that the family was under a tremendous amount of stress and that each member of the family had their individual issues that caused additional amounts of stress. Robert had his new gas station and the problems that they always presented. Kathy was trying to set up a bookkeeping and payroll system for Robert. Helen was in ever-increasing pain with her back. Bill had been out of work for a very long time with no prospects in sight. Colleen had her divorce, and Carrie and David were experiencing money problems and fought more often than not about his infidelity. All these normal everyday problems, compounded by having a mother who had acute Alzheimer's, which grew worse day by day, seemed more than anyone could handle.

Helen looked at Bill and then spoke up. "I think so too. If she needs it, let her have it."

Helen would never speak up against Bill anyway, thought Carrie. And if she did, he'd tell her how stupid she was, as he always had. No one knew as much as Bill, at least, as far as he was concerned.

Carrie recalled getting mad and speaking up. "Wait a minute here. I think you're confusing need with want. I'm not saying Colleen shouldn't get the money, but if she wanted to, she could get more out of Mark. She told me she just didn't want to go to court to fight him for it. I think she feels it would be easier to borrow from Mom." She paused for a moment and continued. "Besides, she doesn't have to buy a house. She could rent one for a while. This is Mom's money we would be lending out, and none of us has any idea how much will be needed for her care in the future. It doesn't feel right to deplete her funds when she may be in need of them in a short time."

Robert interjected. "But she claims she can only get this great deal on this house now, not later." It was clear to Carrie that he was in favor of giving Colleen the money.

"The house is only ten thousand dollars less than it would normally be. It's not like she's getting the house at a steal," Carrie added.

"If she needs the money, I think she should have it," Bill said again with a fresh drink in his hand.

Carrie wondered if this was Bill's way of setting a precedent for when it was his turn to ask for something.

"I agree," added Robert.

"Okay, I'm outvoted, so I'll concede, but I don't think anyone should be lent or given anything until we find out more regarding Medicare and the cost of nursing homes for Mom." Carrie rubbed away the beads of condensation on the outside of her glass with her fingertips as she finished talking.

"She needs it by next week. Let's just go ahead and get an IOU from her, which she offered to have recorded." Robert smiled his sly but attractive smile. "Is that agreed?"

"Yeah," Helen added.

"Is there anything else to discuss?" Robert asked while looking directly at Carrie.

Carrie knew Robert expected her to bring up the issue of the twenty-six hundred dollars. Carrie wanted to but tightened her stomach, clenched her jaw, and forced herself to keep quiet.

The meeting was ended, and everyone headed home. Carrie recalled wondering what was next with Maggie growing worse every day. Maybe that was exactly what they were waiting for, she thought. Something tragic. Maybe they were waiting for Maggie to burn down the house while she was in it, since she was constantly burning holes in her clothes and the furniture. *I guess if Mom and her belongings went up in flames, the siblings wouldn't need to concern themselves further.* She was aware that she was an alarmist, but still she felt a sense of disgust with her siblings.

CHAPTER
TWENTY-NINE

Detective Chavez slid into the driver's seat of his vehicle, retrieved his cell phone from his belt, and flipped open the top to check if any calls or messages had come in while he had been inside the crime-lab building. He noticed a missed call from Amy Newhouse, the gal who prepared the polygraphs for all his cases. He pushed the Callback button and listened to the beeps as the phone dialed the number. He closed the car door so no one would overhear anything said.

"Amy Newhouse speaking."

"Hi, Amy. Detective Chavez here. I see you called me thirty-five minutes ago."

"Yes, I did. I wanted you to know that Mrs. Carrie Stern passed her polygraph."

Okay, that and two fifty will get me a cup of coffee, he thought but didn't say in order not to offend Amy. "Did she seem extremely nervous while she was answering the questions you put to her?"

"Yes, she did. But that's pretty normal for someone so young and never having experienced a polygraph test before. So no, not anything out of the ordinary."

"Okay. Thanks for your call, Amy."

"Sure, no worries," she said before ending the conversation.

Detective Chavez closed the top of his flip phone while repeating Amy's last comment. "No worries." *When had "no problem" become "no worries"?* he thought as he put his phone away and started the car. He wondered what he had missed during the transition of that bit of slang and what else he might have missed with his all-consuming job.

He dismissed the thoughts as he drove his car toward the exit of the underground garage.

He drove for thirty minutes before arriving at Ted Wagner's small home just outside the city limits. The paint on the house had once been white but was now grayish and peeling from age and weather. The house appeared dilapidated and rundown. The detective guessed the house must have been fifty to sixty years old. He looked up at the roof and noticed that the missing shingles outnumbered those that remained sitting on top of the weathered plywood board beneath. The weeds that grew around the entire house were tall, dry, brittle, and thick enough to almost hide the uneven wooden porch, which held one old and timeworn rocking chair. It was something out of a Hollywood scene, he thought, as he approached the rickety screen door, which hung loosely on its hinges. He opened the screen carefully, hoping it would stay attached, at least, until after he was done with his business at the house. He knocked and waited.

The door opened, and Mr. Wagner stood in front of him wearing dirty overalls, no shirt, and a beer in the hand that had not opened the door.

"Hello, are you Mr. Wagner?"

"Yes, sir."

"I'm Detective Estevan Chavez." He flashed his gold badge then tucked it away in his suit pocket. "We spoke on the phone earlier."

"Yes, Detective, I remember. Would you like to come in?"

Detective Chavez hesitated to answer but knew he would have to venture inside whether he wanted to or not. As he reluctantly entered the home, he wondered if the inside of the home was as neglected as the outside appeared to be.

"Thank you," he said unenthusiastically as the musty smell from inside wafted into his nose, making his nostrils wince with disgust.

There was a half inch of debris lying on top of what was once carpeting but was now mostly threadbare, with huge holes here and there, surrounded by threads striking their poses every which way. The dirt was thick beneath the worn carpet, and the smell of dirty dog became stronger and stronger as he ventured further into the home. He acknowledged the cause of the smell when he noticed a large, lazy black dog sitting in front of the filthy broken-down couch.

He headed for the kitchen table, which sat off to the left side of the room, hoping that it was a little cleaner than any other item in the room appeared to be. He pulled out a chair, and Mr. Wagner followed his lead and sat across from him.

"Mr. Wagner, I understand you are employed by Robert Mulligan at one of his gas stations. Is that correct?"

"Yes, sir."

"How long have you worked for Mr. Mulligan?"

"I've been employed with Mr. Mulligan for about four years now."

"What position do you hold?"

"I'm assistant manager there." He smiled as if displaying a sense of pride in his title.

"Do you recall your day last Monday?"

"Yes, sir."

"Can you tell me about that day?" Detective Chavez pulled his notebook and Montblanc pen from his jacket pocket.

"Yes, sir. I arrived at the station at approximately five thirty. It was a little earlier than usual, but Mr. Mulligan wanted some extra cleanup work done that day."

"Was Mr. Mulligan there when you arrived?"

"No. He arrived a few minutes after me. We opened the station and started cleaning up in the work bays first thing."

"Did Mr. Mulligan stay at the station all day?"

"Well, kinda."

"Can you explain that for me? I'm not sure how to interpret 'kinda.' Did he stay around all day or not?"

"Mr. Mulligan, being the owner and all, comes and goes all the time. He always lets me or another employee know when he leaves and when he gets back though."

"Can you recall what occurred on Monday?"

"Yes, sir. Mr. Mulligan started cleaning but left shortly after we started. He said he had to go get some cleaning solution for the oil on the floor of the work bays."

"Do you recall what time he left?"

"No, sir, it was just a little after we started cleaning though."

"What about the rest of the day?"

"Like I said, Mr. Mulligan, being the owner and all, would come and go as he pleased. I didn't always know when he was gone, since there are a couple other fellows who work there. But he'd always let someone know he was leaving."

"So you don't know where he went when he left on Monday morning?"

"He said he was going to get some cleaning solution. That's all I know. I don't question the boss, if you know what I mean." He let out a short chuckle.

"Do you know when he returned?"

"No, not specifically. I was busy cleaning and organizing. Trying to get it done before we got too busy."

Detective Chavez took notes but wondered why Mr. Wagner didn't clean and organize in his own home. The smell of filth was repugnant, and he couldn't wait to get out of there.

"Was there anyone else present during this time? Another employee or customer?"

"No, sir. Just me and Mr. Mulligan."

"Have you ever been arrested, Mr. Wagner?"

"No, sir. I keep a clean record with the law. My daddy taught me to stay away from situations I had no control over."

There's that word again, he thought as he reached inside his jacket pocket for his business card. "Clean" didn't seem to be a word Mr. Wagner fully understood, or least exercise with any regularity at home. He handed the card to Mr. Wagner and got up from the chair. As he pushed it back toward the table, he could feel the grimy, oily residue on the top of the wooden chair, which had presumably accumulated over the years of dirty hands touching the chair never having been cleaned. He was anxious to leave.

"Do you take any medications that might affect your memory?"

"No, sir." He smiled.

"Thank you, Mr. Wagner. I appreciate your cooperation. Call me if you have any questions or remember anything you think I should know."

Mr. Wagner followed him to the front door. "Sure will, Detective."

Detective Chavez felt a light breeze as he exited the house but knew it wouldn't be enough to make him feel clean again. That would take a shower for him and the cleaners for his suit. *Man, how do people live like that?* he thought as he got into his car.

CHAPTER
THIRTY

The blinking light on his answering machine alerted Detective Chavez that messages awaited, so he hit the Message button as he sat at his desk and listened intently.

"Message 1. Sent at five forty-one p.m.," stated the female voice.

"Hi, Estevan, how about dinner at my house Saturday night?" said a sweet female voice. "Call me back, and let me know if you can make it." *Click*.

"Message 2. Sent at six thirty-eight p.m."

"Ah, yeah, Detective Chavez. This is Chet Malik. I have the DNA info you wanted. Give me a call in the a.m." Click.

"Damnit," said Detective Chavez loudly.

"Problem, Detective?" queried an autotheft investigator named Harvey, sitting several desks away.

"That lab rat knows I'm waiting for this information. Now I'll have to wait until tomorrow to get it."

"Yeah, those technicians don't seem to understand that homicide detectives don't sleep."

"Yeah, we're not like autotheft investigators who only work nine to five," he chided in friendly return.

The detective turned on his computer to check for e-mails that might have been sent, almost hoping that Chet Malik would have had enough sense to send a report via e-mail, especially since he hadn't reached the detective by phone. He noted nothing of importance and shut it down.

He'd have no choice but to wait until Chet Malik started work in the morning to find out what information he possessed.

"Aren't you working late, Harvey? It's past five o'clock, ya know."

"Getting ready to go. Have a good evening, Detective," said the auto theft detective as Detective Chavez grabbed his briefcase and left the room.

CHAPTER
THIRTY-ONE

Carrie had finally slept a few hours, even though it was late when she had gotten to sleep. She felt better than she had in the last couple of days, but she was still experiencing the effects of sleep deprivation. Or was it that her brain was having trouble coping with being in jail? She wasn't sure but realized that she was not operating at full capacity. She didn't want to believe that she would have to stay in jail for any length of time, but that was exactly what was happening as the days passed by. This was her third full day here, and her fear had subsided somewhat but not completely. What she feared she wasn't quite sure. Was it her fellow pod mates or being framed for a crime she didn't commit or her absence from her estranged husband and children? The husband wasn't a big deal, she thought. He was already absent from her and the children's life, but she wondered how he was dealing with the children and his new girlfriend. He had better not allow the young hussy to be around her children, she thought with anger. Her temperature rose with the thought of it. They had been going through enough without some blond bimbo attempting to steal a married man away from his family then hanging around and kissing up to small children to win the affection of her boss and lover. *Damnit*, she thought, *this entire situation stinks.*

"Stern, roll call!" yelled the officer on duty. "Get your backside out of bed like everyone else. Unless of course you'd rather be in solitary for twenty-four hours?"

Carrie jumped out of bed and stood at the foot of the bunk. She hated being here. *What on earth would it be like in solitary?* she thought.

She consumed the entire contents of the food tray: oatmeal, toast, sausage, and one egg. Her stomach bulged, but she felt satisfied. She got up to put her tray into the food cart. As she approached the cart, she felt warm breath on the back of her neck. Before she could turn to see who it was, someone whispered in her ear. "You got a nice ass, girl."

She immediately turned and saw a white woman with mousy brown hair and crooked teeth smiling at her. Carrie's skin felt suddenly dirty. She put her tray away and walked away as fast as she could. She said nothing simply because she didn't know what to say but was offended by the comment and what she assumed was some sort of attempt to be inappropriately personal with her.

Carrie walked over to the officer's desk. "Is it possible to schedule an exercise session in the yard this morning?"

"Let me look at the book." The officer flipped through several pages. "Sure, in an hour, for thirty minutes. You want it?"

"Yes, please." Carrie glanced at the clock on the wall. She wanted to make sure she was exactly on time so that her scheduled time wouldn't be wasted by her nonattendance. She was aware that she needed to work out. It would help her sleep as well, she thought. "Is there any task you can assign me to today? I really need to keep busy."

"No. Sorry, Stern. You haven't been here long enough to get assigned to anything, but don't worry, if you stick around, we'll find something for you do to. Clean toilets or mop floors." The officer gave a small laugh.

"Okay, thanks." Carrie walked back to her bunk to count the minutes before she'd be able to work off some energy in the yard. She resumed her supine position on the thin mattress, closed her eyes, and let her mind wander.

Carrie recalled the phone call that had pretty much ended her close relationship with her sister. She recalled how Helen had been uncharacteristically assertive. She must have been drinking a lot of hard liquor with Bill that day, since she was usually mild-mannered and easygoing without alcohol.

"You know, Carrie, I don't think it's very nice of you to tell Robert that I'm a thief." Helen had immediately raised her voice. It seemed her anger had been primed before she dialed the phone.

Whoa, she had thought. Helen had never been aggressive, and now all of a sudden, she was jumping on Carrie. "I didn't exactly say that, Helen." She remembered responding.

"Robert said you are upset because I won't sign an IOU. I think it's pretty bad when you don't trust your own sister."

"Well, Helen, I did trust you. I trusted you to deposit the money that was found in Mom's closet, and you didn't do it. It's been over four months." Carrie recalled that she had tried to put her feelings into gentle words for Helen. Carrie felt that Helen was like a little girl who had never had to be independent or fend for herself. Helen had married Bill when she was nineteen, and he was all she had ever known. He was fifteen years older than she, and he told her what to do, how to do it, and when to do it. He ruled the roost and Helen, in every shape and form, and she simply followed his orders.

"Why don't you just call me a thief to my face?" she yelled at Carrie.

"Helen is a bit upset." Bill's voice was now at the other end of the phone, clearly on a second line. "You know, Carrie, it's a little unreasonable of you to ask Helen to sign an IOU in her condition."

"I don't think it is, Bill. All I am asking for is an IOU, not repayment at this point in time. And I'm not sure any of this has to do with Helen's medical condition." Carrie was feeling her own anger rising within.

Bill's voice grew louder with each sentence. "You're being extremely inconsiderate and self-centered. You must think you run the show with your brother and sisters. You're the only one who didn't want to help Colleen out, and now you're coming down on Helen."

Carrie recalled hearing Helen in the background yelling at the top of her lungs. Bill stopped to tell her to settle down before continuing with Carrie. Carrie assumed Helen had hung up her line and it was Bill she was communicating with now.

"Can't you see how you're upsetting Helen with all this nonsense?"

"Wait a minute, Bill. I'm not out to upset anyone. I am simply trying to look out for my mother's welfare, since she can't do it herself."

Bill interrupted. "Sure, Carrie, since when have you ever cared about anyone else?"

"You know, Bill, Helen wouldn't have had to use Mom's money if you would get off your rear end and get a job." Carrie remembered feeling cornered by Bill's comments and had become defensive.

"Oh, now I'm to blame. Are you calling me a thief too? Bill covered the receiver and told Helen to go take a Valium. But Helen was yelling hysterically over his instructions to her. She was yelling at Carrie, not at Bill.

"I'm not calling anyone a thief, Bill. I just wish that Helen had talked to her siblings about her needs before she chose to use Mom's money for herself, instead of depositing it in Mom's account."

"Are you so afraid that the money won't get repaid? After all these years, you feel you have to resort to slander and tell your brother and sister that Helen stole the money. Helen has done a lot for your mother lately, and I'm sure if we had asked to borrow the money, your mother would have lent it to us."

Carrie thought she heard the sound of liquid and ice being sipped. She decided to try and answer Bill's ramblings.

"I'm not sure that's true, Bill. Mom is so confused that she wouldn't understand what she was agreeing to anyway. Besides, Mom doesn't know about the money Helen used, and she's still upset about the six thousand dollars she lent you and Helen for your latest mortgage payments. She told me she thought she'd never get it back."

"Well, I'll tell her about the money Helen used. I won't allow you to tattle to one more person, and I'll bet she won't care."

Carrie heard him take another drink.

"You do what you must, Bill, but I don't think you should upset Mom with any of this. Don't you think she's confused and upset enough?"

"We'll see. I'll call her right now." And he hung up.

Carrie quickly dialed her mother's number to see if he had called her. The line was busy.

"Shit." She looked up and noticed David had been standing nearby, probably because of the shouting which she was sure the whole house could hear.

"What's up? Are you okay?" David had asked.

"Yeah, I'm fine. Actually, I'm glad it's finally out. I feel better, but poor Mom, she'll be upset when Bill talks to her. She doesn't understand any of this stuff anymore."

Carrie recalled how the call had upset her then, and it still bothered her, and perhaps always would. It was clear to her now that the call had been the final blow that exploded the sibling's relationships forever.

"Stern. It's time."

Carrie was startled by the officer's voice but was pleased to be able to go out to the exercise yard and expend some of the energy she had pent up. She hoped that some strenuous exercise would help her sleep this evening, she thought as she climbed down from the top bunk. It would be a welcome relief from all the memories that were bombarding her mind and tearing at her heart.

CHAPTER
THIRTY-TWO

Detective Chavez arrived at his office early, even before the secretaries, so no coffee had been made. He went to his desk and began straightening up before he settled in to review his file on the Murphy case. He switched on his computer and waited patiently while it booted up.

He noticed a message in his e-mail from the Pawn Shop Detail fellows. He placed the cursor on the message title and clicked the mouse to open it.

"Nothing found thus far in the pawnshops for the Murphy case. Will continue to watch for the rings and keep you updated."

He clicked on the Print button, and once the sheet of paper slid out of the printer, he placed it in the file folder. He reviewed the remaining messages and found nothing useful. He checked his watch. Still too early, he thought, but he picked up the phone and dialed the crime lab anyway.

"You've reached the Crime Lab. If your call was not answered, we are either busy and cannot answer your call at this time, or you have called at a time other than during our normal business hours. Please leave a detailed message, and we will return your call at our earliest convenience." *Beep.*

He placed the receiver back into its cradle and went back to reviewing the file and watching the clock. He noticed Karen walk out of the break room and assumed a pot of coffee would soon be ready. He was ready for a cup and walked over to confirm his assumption and score a fresh cup of coffee.

He returned to his desk with the steaming hot black liquid, set it down, and glanced at the huge wall clock. Seven o'clock. He picked up the phone and hit the Redial button and listened to the varied tones of beeping as the phone dialed the crime lab once more.

"Crime Lab, Becky speaking."

"Great. Detective Chavez here. Is Chet Malik in?"

"I'll connect you to that department."

He heard the phone ring at the other end. It rang a dozen times, but no one answered. He was ready to hang up when he heard a voice.

"Hello," a male voice said in a hurried manner.

"Is Chet Malik in?" he repeated.

"Yes. He's just now coming through the door. Everyone is just arriving. Can I tell him who is calling?"

"Detective Chavez regarding the Murphy case."

"I'll transfer your call, Detective."

Detective Chavez heard the familiar elevator music for less than a minute.

"Chet Malik speaking."

"Yes, Chet, Detective Chavez. I'm calling about the message you left last night. Do you have some information on the Murphy case for me?"

"Yes, Detective. Let me grab the file. Hold on just one minute, please."

He heard the receiver bang against the countertop, then rustling and then Chet again.

"I received the DNA results on the hair evidence late yesterday. The report showed it is definitely male DNA, most likely Caucasian and somewhere in the age range of forty to fifty years old. But take note that the age is always a very rough estimate."

The detective's first thought was, *Oh shit, it's not Carrie. It's a male.* "Okay, at least that gives us more than we had yesterday." He smiled.

Chet's voice interrupted the detective's thoughts. "Do you need a lab tech to accompany you to the suspects in order to get some cheek swabs?"

"Yes, Chet, I do. Any suggestions?"

"Larry is an intern. He knows how to do it." He paused and felt clarification was necessary. "That's the blond kid that was at the front desk the day you came in."

"Yeah, I remember him. That's the kid with the rebellious red streak in his hair, right? Chet, I don't want an intern screwing up my murder case and allowing some asshole murderer to get off."

"No, no. He knows what he's doing, and he is certified to do it. We have a procedure in this particular lab where we have the interns, who are supervised for a six-week period, do those types of procedures. He's done with that, so he's got adequate training."

"Chet, I believe you believe what you're telling me, but this case is on thin ice as it is. Why don't you send me someone with a few years' experience or accompany me yourself?"

"Okay, I'll do it if that's what you prefer. Let me know where and when, and I'll meet you wherever you say."

"I'll call you back in a few minutes."

The detective hung up and opened his file folder to review the ages of the males in the family, since he was convinced that it was most likely a family member who had killed Mrs. Murphy. He realized that he'd have to release Carrie from jail now that the DNA showed it was a male, but he'd take care of that later today, he thought. More important things first. He jotted down the ages of Maggie's son and son-in-law. Both fell into the age range Chet had mentioned, he thought as he called Chet to provide the addresses for both males.

After he hung up the telephone, he decided he'd better take a few minutes to fill out the inmate-release form relating to Carrie's incarceration. He didn't care to open himself to a lawsuit for unlawful detainment. He figured with Carrie being a law student, she'd jump on a situation like that.

He typed the form up quickly and faxed it over to the jail before leaving to meet Chet.

As he hurried to reach his vehicle, his mind raced. He guessed he would have to eliminate the asshole kid, Chuck Presley, as a suspect as well. But maybe not just yet, he thought. He was aware that the age range demonstrated by a DNA sample was sometimes wrong; actually, it occurred more often than not. Maybe he wouldn't dismiss the smart-ass kid just yet. Although, none of the prints found had matched the teenager's prints. And there was no doubt the kid's prints had found their way into the state databases. He still wasn't ready to dismiss him as a suspect. No, not just yet, he thought.

CHAPTER
THIRTY-THREE

Carrie ate her lunch and watched as the female who had warmed her neck after breakfast put her tray away. She waited until her admirer walked away from the area before getting up to place her food tray in the cart. She continued to watch the dirty blond when she saw her turn and wink in Carrie's direction. She tried her best to stay away from everyone, but this female was doing her best to flirt regardless of the distance Carrie put between herself and everyone else. Carrie didn't worry as long as she was in the pod with the officer present; however, the showers were her biggest worry. That was where any offensive contact went undetected by the officers on duty. She would do everything she could to avoid this woman if at all possible.

Carrie walked over to the officer's desk.

"Is it possible to get some more time in the exercise yard?"

"Sorry, Stern, you've had yours. There's no space open for the rest of the day. You want to schedule for tomorrow?"

"Yes, please."

"How about an hour in the morning?"

"Thank you. That would be great."

Carrie reluctantly walked over to her bunk. She was tired of spending all her time lying on that bunk and thinking. It served only one purpose, and that was to keep her away from the other inmates. She closed her eyes, and unwillingly, the memories crept in.

Carrie recalled Christmas time last year. She had promised to take her mother shopping and had pulled into the driveway and walked up to the door to ring the doorbell. She remembered her shock when her mother opened the door in only her slip. Maggie had always been extremely modest. Besides, Maggie didn't know who was at the door when she opened it, so for her to be in her slip was disturbing. Carrie had quickly regained her composure.

"Can't find anything to wear, Mom?"

"I guess." She pulled at her slip. "I can't get this thing on."

Carrie had taken her mother to the bedroom and pulled a dress out of the closet. While assisting her mother with the dress, she wondered when her mother had last bathed. The body odor was strong, and her hair was matted as if it hadn't been combed in weeks.

"I can do that," she insisted in an indignant tone of voice as she tugged at the edge of the dress.

"Okay, Mom, I was just trying to help." Carrie backed away and allowed Maggie to struggle with the clothing.

Maggie resisted any help from anyone. It didn't seem to matter that it was her children who were the ones trying to help instead of a stranger. Carrie recalled that this resistance prevented the children from bringing in outside help. They had tried three times, but a stranger in her house upset Maggie a great deal. In fact, she recalled there wasn't much that didn't upset Maggie in her condition.

Carrie recalled walking into the kitchen to find a swarm of black ants all over the counter. They seemed to be going for the canisters that held the sugar and cookies.

"Mom, have you sprayed for these ants?" Carrie yelled to the back bedroom.

There was no answer, so Carrie walked back to check on her mother.

"Mom, did you know you had ants?"

"Yeah, I guess I do."

"Did you spray for them?"

"Spray for them? What do you mean?" Maggie was confused by simple things, Carrie recalled.

"Spray with ant poison, Mom. Never mind, I'll do it." What once had been a simple chore had now become impossible for Maggie to comprehend.

Carrie went back to the kitchen and looked under the sink for household ant-poison spray. It sat among many bottles and cans. She sprayed along the floorboards and then wiped up the crawling legions of black things on top of the sink and down the sides of the cupboards.

Once the task was complete, they headed for the shopping mall. Maggie was slow to warm up and speak freely but, after sometime had passed mentioned that she was having trouble getting along by herself. Carrie recalled her surprise at her mother's admission. Maggie would, every now and then, mention she was having difficulty but would never say exactly what it was. She did her best to deny and hide that anything was wrong and that she was, in fact, sick.

For no particular reason, Carrie glanced down at her mother's feet once they got into the mall. She noticed Maggie had on two different-colored shoes. Carrie remembered thinking there was no reason to say anything since they were already there; she simply hoped no one else would notice. Carrie had learned to laugh off small things like this. It was her way of dealing with the disease. Besides, Carrie had experienced the anger of her mother many times. Carrie felt like she had to walk on ice around her mother, because if you said something that made Maggie feel less than normal, she would lash out with mean words, and then afterward, she'd be negative all day. Carrie understood that it was the disease that made her combative and volatile, but she also understood that her mother had always been a very negative person and very much an introvert. In fact, Carrie had noticed that Maggie was depressed much of the time as she aged. It might have been the disease, but none of the family was really sure when it had started.

Carrie recalled feeling how difficult it was to watch your mother die a little every day. It was almost as if she was disappearing and the body snatchers were taking over her body. Laughter was the only thing that helped Carrie deal with the calls in the middle of the night, when her mother would inform her that there was a bunch of people in her living room. After a few of those calls, Carrie had learned to simply tell her mother to turn off the television and the people would go away. Carrie thought often about her mother's world and what a frightening place it must be to live in, but it was out of Carrie's control, so she tried not to alarm her mother and acted as if all was normal.

"Did you know that Helen and Bill borrowed money from me?" Maggie informed Carrie.

"Yes, I know, Mom." Carrie had heard this comment many times.

"I don't think they'll pay it back. The other day Helen bought about ten hanging plants for the backyard. How can they afford to do that?"

"I'm sure they'll pay you back when they can, Mom. I guess Bill still hasn't found a job."

"No, he's still at home. They're redoing the entire backyard."

"Are they?" Carrie had heard all about this from Robert and really didn't care to hear about it again, but she was sure she would hear about it many times. Maggie now repeated things over and over. Carrie tried to understand since Maggie didn't have anyone to talk to except her children and her world didn't involve anything else but her children.

Carrie recalled she had given up trying to find Christmas gifts for Maggie to give and decided that gift cards would be easier. They picked up several and headed for home.

Carrie prayed silently as she drove home. She had sworn to herself that she'd never put any of her family through this. If she ever thought she had Alzheimer's, she'd take the matter into her own hands.

She tossed on her bunk and wished lights-out was closer. She still had dinner and two hours' recreation time to get though before she could even make an attempt at sleeping. She didn't want to remember anymore. Going through it once was enough, she thought. The memories were painful, and she wanted to stop the pain, the hurt, and the nightmare she was experiencing.

"Stern." She heard her name but didn't respond. "Stern, gather your belongings."

She heard what the officer was saying but was confused. *Why would she gather her belongings?* She thought. She sat up and looked at the officer that was speaking.

"Stern, gather your belongings, and report to the door!" yelled the officer.

"I don't understand."

"A release has been faxed over by the detective bureau. You want to get outta here or not?"

"Yeah." Her motions suddenly contained urgency. She grabbed her personal items and threw them in her black net bag. She reached the door in minutes; she looked back briefly and noticed the dirty blond blow her a kiss good-bye, but she ignored it. She felt relieved that she would not have to endure the woman's advances any longer. An officer waited for her on the other side of the door. It slid open. She hurried out.

"Stern, come with me, and we'll get you processed."

"Do you know why I'm being released?"

"Stern, you need to ask your attorney. They don't tell us much. Just be glad you're being released."

"That's an understatement," she said as she dutifully followed the officer down the hallways. She smiled to herself as she visualized getting home and giving her kiddos hugs and kisses until they begged her to stop. And kicking her useless, unfaithful husband out the door. *Thank you God for allowing me to get out of this place*, she thought as she followed the officer through the locked doors. It was hard for her to contain her excitement at being released. She bounced as she walked and had a wide grin on her face. *Life would be different from now on*, she thought. *I'm going take control of my own life from now on.* Carrie felt strength and determination flow through her body, making her feel new and replenished.

CHAPTER
THIRTY-FOUR

The detective and lab technician stood at the St. Claire front door waiting. The detective knocked a second time. No answer.

"Let's go to the Mulligan residence and see if we get better results," he said to Chet as he turned away from the door.

Chet said nothing. He went to his vehicle ready to follow the detective. Once they arrived at the Mulligan home, he approached the front door again carrying what looked like a tackle box, which held his testing supplies.

Detective Chavez had already knocked and was waiting for a response. The door opened, and Robert stood there.

"Detective Chavez," he said. It sounded more like a question than a statement.

"Mr. Mulligan, may we come in?"

"Yes." He opened the screen door.

Detective Chavez held his hand out toward Chet. "This is Chet Malik from the crime lab." Chet bowed his head slightly in acknowledgement but said nothing.

"Hi," replied Robert as he backed away from the door slightly.

Detective Chavez stopped just inside the door and turned to face Robert. "We've come to request that you provide us with a DNA sample. This is normal procedure in a case like this. It helps eliminate those individuals who had nothing to do with the murder." He paused to allow the information to be absorbed by Robert. He continued after thirty seconds. "It's nothing invasive. We don't have to draw blood or anything like that. All I need is a saliva sample. You would only need to take a cotton swab and rub it gently inside your mouth. It's pretty simple."

He paused and waited for a response from Robert. Several seconds passed. He could tell that Mr. Mulligan was thinking the request over and probably the possible implications of it in his mind.

"If you're innocent, there's no reason not to provide the sample," continued the detective. "However, if you refuse, we can get a court order to obtain it, so either way, we'll get a sample. You decide how hard you want to make it."

Robert snapped out his silence with a raised voice. "I'm innocent, so whatever you need is fine with me."

Chet set his tackle box on the half-round table, which stood just off the entryway. He opened it, took out an envelope, which held two gloves, put them on, then removed a clear plastic vial that held a cotton swab at the end of a wooden stick approximately six inches long. He removed the stopper from the vial and was careful not to touch the cotton tip to anything that might contaminate it then handed the wooden end to Mr. Mulligan. "Just open your mouth, and rub the inside of your cheek with the cotton tip," he instructed.

Robert did as instructed and handed the wooden stick back to Chet, who was again careful not to touch the tip to the sides of the vial as he slid it in. He capped it, placed a sticky strip around the top, and put his initials, date, and time on it. He verified the information with Robert and then commenced to write Robert's name and date of birth on the horizontal sticker on the side of the vial and requested that Robert put his initials next to the information.

"I have a consent form for you to sign as well, please." Chet handed the piece of paper to Robert, who quickly signed his name and handed it back.

"How long does it take to get the results?" Robert asked.

"Approximately three days, sometimes longer." Chet folded the paper in half. He put the vial inside of a plastic bag he had taken from his kit and then slid the consent form into a pocket on the outside of the bag.

"Thank you for your cooperation, Mr. Mulligan." Detective Chavez said as they turned to leave.

"Detective? Do I need to get a lawyer or anything?"

"Not if you're innocent. Besides, you're not under arrest, haven't been given your rights, and I haven't interrogated you. We've just had a friendly conversation prior to this. No, you don't need to get a lawyer, but you're free to do so if you wish." Detective Chavez shut the screen door behind him and walked to his car.

"Let's try Mr. St. Clair again," he said to Chet before opening the door to his vehicle.

Chet followed the detective the few short blocks between the two homes.

They stood at the front door once more. Detective Chavez rang the doorbell and knocked several times on the door. They waited. He knocked again, harder this time. The door opened, and Bill stood in front of them in his boxer shorts.

"Detective," he said in surprise.

"May we come in, Mr. St. Clair?"

"Yes. Come in. I'll go put some clothes on." Bill left the door open for the two men to enter and scurried down the hall to get some clothes. He returned within minutes and was dressed more appropriately this time.

"This is Chet Malik from the crime lab. Would you mind if we stepped into your kitchen?"

They stepped into the kitchen, which was off the entryway, and Chet set his tackle box on the round wooden table. The faint smell of dirty cat litter filled the air. Detective Chavez took his white linen handkerchief out of his suit pocket and held it to his nose. "Sorry. I'm allergic to cats. I wasn't aware that you had cats."

"She's a new addition to the family," Bill responded but made no effort to remove the object that was emitting the offensive odor.

Detective Chavez removed his handkerchief. "I'm here to request that you consent to giving us a DNA sample."

Before he could continue, Bill interrupted. "Why do you need that from me?"

"As I was going to explain, it's normal procedure in a murder case. We don't know what happened, so it helps us eliminate those persons who had nothing to do with the homicide. It's a nonevasive procedure. No blood or urine samples. Just a simple cheek swab." He immediately raised the linen cloth to his face again. His eyes were beginning to redden, and he had to clear his throat several times.

"No," Bill said adamantly. "I didn't do anything wrong, so why would I give a DNA sample?"

Detective Chavez removed the handkerchief again. "Well, if you're truly innocent, why not give it?"

"No," Bill said loudly. "What about innocent until proven guilty?" he stammered.

"I'm afraid you're mixing the presumption of innocence with the right of the investigator to obtain evidence that might determine innocence or guilt, Mr. St. Claire." Detective Chavez was trying his best to maintain a friendly tone up until this point. However, the irritation he was feeling from the allergic reaction to the cat was not helping his attitude one bit.

The three of them stood looking at each other for almost thirty seconds.

"Okay, Mr. St. Claire, if you refuse to give up a DNA sample, I'll have no choice but to get a court order for the sample." He coughed several times. "Any way you wish to handle this, Mr. St. Claire, one way or the other, we'll get your DNA sample." Now he was pissed.

"I'm not giving up anything, Detective, so do what you must." Bill walked to the door and opened it, meaning it to be a clear invitation for them to leave.

"Good afternoon," said Chet as he followed Detective Chavez out.

The door shut loudly.

Before entering their vehicles, Detective Chavez stopped and turned to address Chet.

"Achoo, achoo, achoo, achoo. Damn cats." He blew his nose. "Sorry, Chet. I'll need you to come back with me once I get the court order. Probably later this afternoon."

"Yeah, sure, Detective. Just give me a call when you have the court order."

"Thanks, Chet."

The detective entered his car while sneezing numerous times.

CHAPTER
THIRTY-FIVE

Detective Chavez returned to his office to type up the request for a court order for nontestimonial identification, provided for under Rule 41.1 of the Rules of Criminal Procedure. It was a simple form, much like the forms requesting a search warrant. He carefully typed in his reasons for thinking the DNA sample was necessary and why from this particular person.

As he finished the typing, he glanced at his wristwatch. It was nearly noon, and now the problem would be to catch the judge before he went to lunch or between cases. His mind raced, thinking of several things he still needed to accomplish. Helen, he thought, he needed to question Helen.

He dialed Officer Osmond, who answered immediately. "Jeff. Detective Chavez here."

"Hi, Detective, what can I do for you?"

"Jeff, what's your schedule like this afternoon?"

"Right now, I'm clear. What do you need?"

"I need you to pick up Helen St. Claire for questioning."

"Okay, I can do that. Where and when?"

"She usually gets off work around three o'clock. Swing by the Hometown Pharmacy, and ask her to come down to the station. Tell her we need further information. Don't alarm her, and by all means, don't let her call her husband."

"Okay, will do."

The detective hung up and hurried over to the courthouse, which was only two blocks from the police department. He walked into Judge

Marks's polished wood-paneled courtroom with the huge round state seal behind the judge's bench and the state and federal flags on each side.

He noticed the court clerk had vacated her spot next to the judge's bench and the bailiff had left as well. The room was empty except for the vibrations of authority, which permeated the room. He continued through the open door at the far right side of the back wall.

He noticed Judge Marks removing his robe and ready to put on his suit jacket. He was a common-looking middle-aged man, well-dressed and well-liked by the community. It didn't hurt that he was from a very well-to-do family when election time had arrived. He had been elected to three consecutive terms and appeared to love his job and the power it wielded.

The detective cleared his throat loudly in an effort to announce his presence. Judge Marks turned to face him. "Hello, Detective Chavez. What can I do for you this afternoon?" He glanced at his watch. "I only have a couple of minutes, so it needs to be quick if you want it done before I go to lunch."

"It is. I just need a signature on an order for Rule 41-1." He held the document out toward the judge.

"What case is this regarding?" he asked as he took the document and began to scan it.

"It's the Murphy case. The murder of the elderly lady. Poisoning," he reminded the judge.

Silence remained between the two for several minutes while Judge Marks read the documents.

"So you think its family that did it?" He leaned over his desk to retrieve a pen for signing.

"The DNA points to a male in the age range of forty to fifty years old. Both males in the family fall into that category." He stood with his hands in front of him, and his fingers intertwined.

"Yeah, well, that age range can sometimes trick you. I'm sure you're aware of that fact though." He scribbled his signature at the bottom of the paper and handed it back to the detective.

"Yes, Your Honor, I realize some of the DNA information isn't as reliable as other elements of the DNA profile, but it's all I have to go on right now. I haven't completely eliminated the other male suspects." He took the document and turned to leave. "Thanks. Have a good lunch." He hurried out of the door he had entered through.

He dialed Chet's cell phone as he walked back to his office. He got a recording.

"Yeah, Chet. I need you to meet me at the Caverns address that we were at this morning. I'll be there in thirty minutes. Call me if that's a problem. Otherwise, I'll see you in thirty."

He flipped the phone closed and headed for the copier to make a copy to be given to the individual being ordered to submit to its demands.

"Okay, Bill St. Claire," he said out loud as the copier light scanned the document, "it's showtime."

CHAPTER
THIRTY-SIX

When Detective Chavez pulled up to the St. Claire residence, he noticed the garage door was moving in an upward direction. He watched for a second as it continued to rise. He exited his vehicle and walked to the left side of the garage door. He saw a pale-blue older-model Cadillac slowly inch from its resting place. The driver's window was up, so he reached out and knocked on it.

Mr. St. Claire appeared startled. He brought the moving vehicle to a halt in an effort to ascertain who had tapped on his window. He rolled down the glass barrier. "Oh, Detective. I didn't see you there."

"Yeah, I know." He smiled. "Would you mind getting out of the car and talking with me?"

Bill didn't reply but turned off the engine and opened the door to exit. He moved slowly and appeared disturbed by the detective's unexpected appearance.

Chet's vehicle pulled up and parked directly behind the Cadillac, blocking the driveway.

The detective was pleased to see Chet showing such forethought, or at the very least, blocking the driveway by accident. One way or the other, it prevented Mr. St. Claire's exit.

Bill stood facing Detective Chavez as he stood in the opened door of the car holding on to the door's frame.

"I have a court order here, Mr. St. Claire." He handed the document to Bill. "This allows me to collect a DNA swab from you without your consent. How would you like to handle this? We can do this with your cooperation or without—it's your choice." The detective pulled his handcuffs from his back pocket and held them up for Bill to clearly see them.

Chet laid his tackle box on the ground next to Detective Chavez, opened it, and removed a plastic bag containing the DNA swab kit. He put on a set of gloves and removed the cotton-tip applicator. He handed it to Bill.

Bill reluctantly took the swab, rolled it inside his left cheek as instructed to do, and handed it back to Chet. Meanwhile, Detective Chavez placed the handcuffs back into their case.

Chet sealed the vial, labeled it, replaced it in the bag, and asked Mr. St. Claire to initial the bag once it was sealed and labeled with appropriate information.

Detective Chavez had been viewing the contents of Bill's car while Chet obtained the swab. He saw no suitcase or anything else that might provide a clue as to where Bill was headed when he had approached the vehicle.

"Where are you going?" he asked Bill.

"To the gym."

"Mind if I take a look in your trunk?"

Bill didn't respond verbally but leaned inside the car to release the trunk lock.

Detective Chavez walked behind the car to view the inside of the trunk. He saw nothing suspicious. "Okay. Let me remind you to stick around town while this investigation is ongoing."

"Sure. No problem."

"Thank you for your cooperation, Mr. St. Claire." His voice had a tone of satisfaction in it.

Detective Chavez and Chet Malik walked down the driveway. The detective turned toward Chet and pointed to the tackle box. "Stat."

"Understood," Chet replied as he entered his vehicle.

CHAPTER
THIRTY-SEVEN

It was a little past three thirty when Detective Chavez got back to his office to find Officer Osmond waiting for him.

"Mrs. St. Claire is in interview room 5. Videotape is ready to go."

"Thanks, Jeff."

Detective Chavez walked straight to room 5 and entered. "Good afternoon, Mrs. St. Claire."

"Hello, Detective." Helen sat with her back to the concrete block wall with a small table in front of her and a one-way window to her right.

Detective Chavez grabbed the remaining chair and positioned it one foot in front of Helen. He pushed the table a foot toward the left until it rested against the wall and gave him more open access to Helen. He recited the Miranda rights warning to her.

"Do you understand the rights I've just read to you, Mrs. St. Claire?"

"Yes."

"And do you agree to speak with me at this time?"

"Yes. But I don't understand why I'm here. Haven't I answered all your questions already?"

"Yes, you have, but I'll explain it all to you in a minute. I will be recording this conversation on videotape, since we will have to ask you to sign a statement when we're done here. Is that all right with you?"

"Yes, I guess so." She fidgeted in her seat.

"Mrs. St. Claire, I've asked you down here because I have a feeling you have more information to share with me."

"Like what?" she asked innocently.

"Like what really happened to your mother."

"I don't know anything more than what I've already told you."

"I think you do, Mrs. St. Claire."

"What are you suggesting, Detective?"

"I think you know who killed your mother." He paused for a moment, but when Helen said nothing, he continued. "You owed her a lot of money, and you didn't like taking care of her."

Helen interrupted him. "No—no," she stammered. "I didn't mind taking care of her." She lowered her voice somewhat. "But yes, we did owe her a lot of money." Helen clutched her purse tightly in her lap.

"Helen. May I call you Helen?" He scooted his chair several inches closer to her.

"Yes, I guess so." She crossed her legs at the ankles.

"Helen, several years ago, my father became very ill, and I had to care for him for a very long time, and it was very hard on me, since I had to work full-time and still be a caregiver. I know how terribly hard it is, both mentally and physically. There were times when I wished the situation would end." He paused for several seconds in an effort to let Helen take in what he had said. "Can you relate to how I might have felt?" His voice had a gentleness to it.

"Yes."

"Were there times when you wished the situation regarding your mother's condition were different?"

"Yes, of course. No one would wish for that situation. It was terribly stressful."

"Were there times when you wished it would end?"

She paused before answering. "Well, sort of, but I would never hurt my mother," she said adamantly.

"What would you say if I told you we have your fingerprints at the scene?" His voice remained gentle.

She paused, took in a deep breath, then responded. "Well, I guess my prints would be there because I took care of my mother and was at her house a lot. At least once a week, if not more."

"Yes, I understand that, but we have your prints on what we suspect to be the murder weapon." The lies began.

"What?" Her voice was louder than it had been. "What murder weapon? There was no murder weapon." She shifted in her chair and hugged her purse tightly to her bosom.

"Helen, your mother was poisoned. She was given tainted food that contained the *Clostridium botulinum* toxin in it." He paused and noticed her look of question. "Helen, your mother died of botulism as a result of what was fed to her with the intent to kill her." He noticed Helen's look of question disappear and then understanding take its place.

Helen breathed deeply again and then placed her hand over her mouth as if surprised by the information.

"But then you knew all about this, didn't you, Helen?" He scooted his chair closer so that his knees were within centimeters of Helen's.

"No." She made an effort to back away, but her chair was already up against the wall. "I didn't kill my mother," she whispered. Tears began to form in the corner of her eyes.

"Helen, if you were to be convicted of killing your mother, you would spend the rest of your life in prison. Are you aware of that?" He spoke softly.

"No." Helen began to cry. She reached inside a side pocket of her purse and retrieved a tissue from its cellophane package.

"Helen, did you kill your mother?" he asked her gently but matter-of-factly.

She did not answer.

"Helen, we know you had motive. You owed your mother a lot of money. You were at the house that morning. You and your husband are in a ton of debt, since your husband hasn't worked in over two years, and you tried to frame your younger sister because she stands to inherit more than any of the other siblings. That's a pretty accurate picture, isn't it, Helen?"

"I didn't kill my mother." Her tears slid down her cheeks, and she could hardly catch her breath now.

"Helen, do you know who killed your mother?"

Helen shifted in her seat and directed her attention to the solid brick wall to her left and remained silent.

"Helen, if you confess now, I'll ask the prosecutor to request a lighter sentence. Why don't you tell me all about it? You need to help yourself right now." He said this sternly, but still with a hint of compassion.

"You need to talk to Bill," she said quietly with her head hung low.

"Why do I need to talk to Bill, Helen?"

"You need to talk to Bill," she repeated. "He told me what to do," she said very quietly.

"What did he tell you to do, Helen?" He realized he had broken her.

"He said it would be best for everyone." She stopped to blow her nose into the wet tissue. "He said my mother didn't have any quality of life, and neither did we as long as she lived." Helen's voice was still lowered but slightly more audible than before.

"So you fed your mother the chili sauce that killed her?" It sounded like a statement but was really a question.

"No." She wiped her wet nose with the back of her hand and wiped the tears with the tissue that was now waded and wet with mucous and salty tears.

"So you just allowed her to eat the chili sauce, Helen?"

"No."

"Okay, Helen, I can understand why you would want your life back, so just tell me how it happened." The detective's voice was soft and understanding.

"Bill."

"Bill what, Helen?"

"Bill fed it to her. He told me to go to the house afterward to discover the body and call 911."

The detective smiled inwardly. He had accomplished what he had set out to do but didn't let it show outwardly. He still had a lot of information to get out of Helen.

"Where did Bill get the tainted food, Helen?"

"He found the can of chili sauce when he had to clean out his elderly Aunt's home after she passed away." She stopped.

"Okay, then what happened?" he coaxed.

"He brought it home and sat at the computer researching it. He told me that the company who made it had recalled it because it had the botulinum toxin in it. He looked up how to handle it and how to dispose of it." She paused and fumbled with her purse for more tissues.

The detective waited patiently for her to continue.

"He said it would be a perfect cure for the situation. He said no one would suspect us, since my mother was so sick and confused."

"I guess Bill didn't count on your mother hitting her head on the counter, making the death appear suspicious, did he?"

"I guess not." She hung her head as she spoke. "He said it didn't matter if she died because she really wasn't in that shell of a body anyway. She actually was dying a day at a time over the course of her disease." She had stopped crying.

"And did you agree with that train of thought?"

"Yes, I guess so. It just seemed so unfair to everybody when she got Alzheimer's. Everybody's life was turned upside down." She stopped to blow her nose once again.

"Helen, did you make any effort to convince Bill that this was the wrong thing to do?"

"No. It seemed like the right thing to do for the sake of my mother. She had no quality of life left, and her condition was affecting everyone else's quality of life." She paused. "Besides, you don't know Bill. Nobody tells Bill he's wrong."

"Did the money you owed to your mother play into your plan?"

"I guess so. I mean, if she was gone, no one would ask for the money to be returned, and Bill said we'd inherit from her and could get caught up on our bills."

Detective Chavez let Helen ramble.

"It's not like her money was being used to give her a better life. She was basically gone. Just an empty body existed. The mother I had known all my life was already gone." Helen began to cry again.

"So you think that was the right thing to do to your mother?"

"Yes, at least, Bill said it was the right thing to do."

"Helen, did you agree with Bill?"

"Yes, I guess I did. At least, it seemed right at the time." She wiped her wet nose with the back of her hand.

"Helen, do you know anything about the rings your mother was missing when you found her?"

"No. I don't know what happened to them. She never took off her jewelry."

"Did Bill say anything about your mother's jewelry to you?"

"No."

"Did you ask Bill about the rings?"

"Yes. He said he had no idea what happened to them."

"Did you question him any further about the rings?"

"Well, I tried, but he refused to discuss it with me."

"Helen, the first day I met you at your mother's house, you told me that you thought Carrie killed your mother. Was she involved?"

"No." She paused for a few seconds. "Bill thought that if Carrie was found guilty, we'd inherit more money from my mom's estate."

"Helen, I'm going to have to take you into custody."

"Okay." She sat still, saying nothing, waiting for the next step.

"Helen, do you know if Bill is at home right now?"

"No." She paused. "I mean, yes, I know if he's home, but no, he's not. He told me this morning that he was going away for a few days. I think he was headed to his aunt's home in Empire. It hasn't sold yet."

"Can you give me the address of his aunt's home?" He pulled a small notebook from his shirt pocket and his favorite black Montblanc pen.

"It's 108 Geyser Drive, in Empire. It's the only bright-pink house in town."

"I'll have a statement of this interview prepared. It won't take long, and then I'll bring it in for your signature. It'll be about thirty minutes. Can I get you something to drink while you wait?"

"Water would be nice." She placed her right hand to her forehead and rested her elbow on her left hand, which sat upon the leather black purse in her lap.

Detective Chavez got up, went to the door, opened it, and requested that the nearest officer bring Mrs. St. Claire some water. "I'll be right back," he said as he left the room, closing the door behind him.

Helen made no response.

He returned after preparing the necessary documentation, along with the arrest warrant, a search warrant of the St. Claire residence, the Empire home, and any cars. He felt grateful for the templates the department had created for use by the detectives. The specific information required for one form could be cut and pasted into another form, making the massive task much quicker than it had been when the detective had first come onto the homicide unit, when it was necessary to type each document separately.

The unit secretary had been busy preparing the statement from the videotape, which she accomplished rather quickly, since she had been a court reporter for fifteen years prior to being hired as the homicide unit secretary.

Detective Chavez was grateful she hadn't gone home yet and didn't mind working a little overtime. The amount of documentation required in any case was sometimes overwhelming. The thought of a defense lawyer convincing the court to throw out the evidence he had worked so hard to get was always in the back of his mind. He knew it was worth taking the time to get the paperwork right.

He took the prepared statement and walked into the interview room to find Helen with her head resting on the concrete brick wall, staring straight ahead at the opposite brick wall. She appeared to be in an apathetic state.

"Are you all right, Mrs. St. Claire?" He set the paperwork on the table and sat down.

"How long will I have to go to prison?" Her voice was shaky, and she hadn't changed her position.

"I'll talk to the prosecutor and see what we can do to lessen your sentence given the fact that you've been so cooperative in this matter. However, I can't make any promises until I speak with the DA's office."

She briefly reviewed the statement that sat in front of her.

When the detective asked her to sign the statement, she did so without any comments or questions.

"Thank you. Now, Mrs. St. Claire, I am going to have one of our female officers come and assist you with the intake process."

He got up from his chair and left the room. He was anxious to locate the judge and obtain signatures on his warrants and then search the St. Claire residence. It was evening, so he'd try the judge's home first.

CHAPTER
THIRTY-EIGHT

Detective Chavez dialed Judge Marks's residence. A female voice answered.

"Hello." It was a sweet, gentle voice.

"Hello. Is this Mrs. Marks?"

"Yes."

"This is Detective Estevan Chavez. Is Judge Marks available?"

"Yes. I'll get him." She set the phone down.

"Yes, Detective, what can I do for you?"

"I have several warrants that I need signatures on, Your Honor."

"Okay. Come over to the house, and we'll see what you've got."

"Okay, be there in twenty minutes." He hung up the phone and felt the adrenaline rush within, starting from his head and flowing to his toes. He knew it was time to get his man, the coldhearted murderer. It was only at this point in time in any murder case that Detective Chavez felt the long hours, the stress of the job, and the low pay that came with the job was worthwhile.

The commute traffic had decreased considerably, since rush hour had long since passed. He parked his car in front of the large yellow house and hurried up the walkway of the judge's home. The door opened before he could employ his normal habit of knocking on every door he stood in front of.

"Hello, Detective." The judge opened the door to allow the detective to enter. "Come in to my study, and we'll see what you have." He reached for the documents the detective held out to him and then led the way into the study, which was the room to the right of the front entry.

Detective Chavez stood quietly as the judge perused the voluminous paperwork.

The judge looked up after a few minutes. "Oh, I'm sorry, Detective, please have a seat."

"Thank you, Judge, but the adrenaline has my motor running, and I'm too wired to sit down." He smiled.

The judge laughed. "Always the excitement about getting your man, right, Detective?"

"Yes, sir."

The judge continued to read on until he'd seen all the warrants.

"So you think your man has taken off to Empire?"

"Yes, at least that's where his wife thinks he is."

"It sounds as if she gave you a lot to go on."

"Yes. She was pretty scared when I told her she could get life in prison. That's when she decided to talk. Thank goodness she didn't decide to lawyer up." He continued to stand resolutely near the entrance to the study, hoping the judge would get on with signing the warrants so he could get going.

"Have you seen the forensic reports regarding the poisoning, and the DNA reports?" the judge inquired as he picked up a pen from the top of the beautiful large mahogany desk but paused, waiting for the detective's response.

"Yes, sir. I've seen the reports. The poisoning has been verified as botulism. We also have verification on the DNA from the hairs found inside the glove. But I'd still like to find Mrs. Murphy's rings and the other items listed on the search warrants. That would make this a good case for the prosecution."

The judge bent over his desk, set the documents down, and signed each one.

"Good luck, Detective." He handed the papers to the detective.

"Thank you, sir."

They both headed toward the front door. The judge opened it for the detective.

"I'll be waiting to hear about the results tomorrow. Take care, Detective."

"Yes, sir. I'll let you know what we find."

The detective walked to his car with a smile. *The SOB is gonna go down,* he thought as he started his car.

Once he arrived at his office, he made copies of the warrants. He was anxious to participate in the search of the St. Claire residence, but not until first thing in the morning. He figured the house would stay as was, since Mrs. St. Claire was in custody and Mr. St. Claire was out of town. Nevertheless, he'd exercise caution and position an officer at the residence overnight to make sure no one entered while he was busy making sure his prime suspect didn't go any further out of town than he already had.

He called Officer Osmond at home to ask if he was interested in assisting with an arrest this evening. He knew he'd have to clear it with the captain first, since it meant overtime for Officer Osmond. It was common knowledge within the station that Officer Osmond wanted to become a detective in the worst way. This would give him some added credibility next time he asked for a transfer to the detective bureau.

He sat at his desk and dialed the Empire Police Department.

"Empire Police, how may I help you?" said a young masculine voice.

"Is your police chief available?"

"Who's calling please?"

"Oh, sorry. This is Detective Estevan Chavez of the Lucerne Police Department. I need to speak with your chief on an urgent matter."

"Sure, Detective, I'll patch you through to his home."

"Thanks." He waited patiently as several types of beeping and buzzing occurred at the other end. He wondered if the Empire Police Department lacked sophistication and, therefore, no elevator music. Before he could answer his own thoughts, a voice with a redneck accent came on the line.

"Yeah, Detective. What can I do for you?"

"Yes, Chief Farley. Hello. I would like to make an arrest of a male murder suspect who is, to my understanding, staying in the home located at 108 Geyser Drive. I'd like to get your department's assistance and ask that you allow me to make the arrest in your jurisdiction."

"Well, sure thing, Detective. When do you want to make the arrest of the ol' boy?"

"This evening. I can be up there in approximately forty-five minutes. I'll bring one officer with me, and if you have a couple to spare, I'd appreciate the assistance."

"Sure thing. We'll be ready for you at the office when you pull into town."

"Great. Thanks for your help."

He hung up the phone then called the captain to clear the use of Officer Osmond. He'd have to explain why he wanted Officer Osmond since there were clearly other officers on duty this evening who could have assisted. He'd tell the captain that Officer Osmond was very familiar with the case and the persons of interest and would be the best choice under the circumstances.

Once he received the okay from the captain, he dialed Officer Osmond's home.

"Hello."

"Yeah, Jeff, Detective Chavez here. Will you assist me with the arrest of Bill St. Claire, who I believe is in Empire tonight?"

"Yes, that would be great. I'll get dressed and be down at the station in no time." He hung up the phone without saying good-bye.

Detective Chavez could understand his excitement. He remembered when he had been on the force for a short while and was asked to assist in the detective unit. Man, that was a great feeling, he recalled.

CHAPTER
THIRTY-NINE

Detective Chavez drove to the tiny redbrick building, which housed the small but adequate police department of Empire. The town consisted of two hundred seventy-three people, four police officers, one police chief, a tiny post office next to the police department, a small grocery store, an ice-cream shop, one gas station, one bed-and-breakfast establishment, one moderately sized trailer park, and about a hundred single-family homes within a small proximity of each other and all within a short walk to the main street. The homes were nothing big or majestic, although the area was. The pine trees that covered the tall mountains in the distance were lush, green, and healthy. The beauty of the mountains with tall, jagged peaks protected the town from brutal weather. It was a beautiful little town in the mountains.

As Detective Chavez got out of his car to approach the glass door of the police department, he could hear the trees rustling in the wind and the creek water rushing over rocks in a nearby creek. He took a deep breath of the clear, crisp air before opening the door. He noticed Officer Osmond pull the patrol car behind his but remained in his car. Detective Chavez walked in and noticed a gray-haired, skinny fellow sitting behind a desk, which appeared to have been well used.

"Hello. I'm Detective Chavez. Are you Chief Farley?" He walked over to the desk as the old fellow rose from the seat slowly, as if having some difficulty moving.

"Yes, sir, I'm Chief Farley. Let's go get your man. I'm ready whenever you are, and I have an officer watching the house. We'll be there to assist if need be, but you fellows can take all the glory, and the paperwork associated with it." He grinned.

"Great. Let's go." Detective Chavez scurried out the door at a rapid pace. He was so close to catching his man he could taste it, he thought.

Detective Chavez drove his unmarked vehicle as Officer Osmond followed. Behind them, a caravan of three more police vehicles from Empire headed in a northerly direction. They quietly drove to the residence in question, without sirens or anything to draw attention from the local people. It was late evening, and most Empire citizens were fast asleep.

The vehicle pulled quietly to the side of the bright-pink home on the dirt road. There were only three homes on the road, but the road continued for another quarter of a mile. At the end of the street stood what appeared to have been an old schoolhouse, which was most probably used many, many years ago.

The officers surrounded the house, positioning themselves at each corner of the home, and made ready their weapons.

Detective Chavez pulled his .357 Mag. from his shoulder holster, knocked hard on the door, and yelled. "Police, open up!" He waited for about thirty seconds, realizing that the occupant had most likely been awakened from sleep. He knocked harder and spoke louder. "Police, open up!" He heard noise from inside as the door handle turned and the door opened slightly.

Detective Chavez pointed his gun at Bill. "Mr. St. Claire, come out peacefully, and no harm will come to you."

Bill opened the door wide and raised his hands in response to the weapon staring him in the face.

"You're under arrest for the murder of Maggie Murphy." Detective Chavez stepped inside, put away his gun, pulled out his handcuffs, and snapped them closed on Bill's wrists.

Officer Osmond now stood at the door watching as Detective Chavez recited the Miranda rights to Bill.

"I want a lawyer," stated Bill.

"You're going to need one. Officer Osmond, put Mr. St. Claire in your car while I search the premises." He flashed the search warrant at Bill before he was led out to the patrol car.

"Sure thing." He gently led Mr. St. Claire through the overgrown front yard to his car.

Detective Chavez went from room to room to find nothing except the cot, sleeping bag, and pillow Bill had been using. He also found a tattered leather travel case, which held a toothbrush, toothpaste, and electric razor in it, but nothing of significance.

As he walked about the old house, he could smell the musty, moldy odor that accompanied a house that had been built close to a hundred years ago. "Achoo, achoo, achoo, achoo, achoo." He reached into his back pocket for his folded linen handkerchief. "Damn allergies," he said as he blew his nose to release the moldy smell from his anterior nasal passage.

Detective Chavez left the house and walked to the back of the home where Bill's Cadillac was parked. He pulled on a fresh pair of gloves and pulled on the door handle. To his surprise, it opened. One of the nice things about living in a small town, he thought as he began to search the car. He didn't see anything obvious, so he proceeded to the glove compartment. He dug through an owner's manual, a flashlight, several maps, and a personal-size tissue package but found nothing of interest. He popped the trunk and searched, finding nothing once again. He was disappointed. He closed up the car and removed his gloves. He then walked over to the patrol car and asked Jeff to place yellow police tape around the perimeter of the home and car then walked over to the police chief.

"Chief Farley, thank you for your assistance."

"Sure thing. Y'all have a good evening." He shook the detective's hand and motioned for his officers to get on with their normal duties.

Detective Chavez headed for his car then changed direction and went to the patrol car.

"Officer Osmond, would you mind taking Mr. St. Claire to the detention center? I'll be right behind you. I've still got a ton of paperwork to do before we start the St. Claire residence search in the morning."

"Sure, anything you need."

"Yeah, I should let you help me with the paperwork so you could see the reality of life as a detective." He laughed.

"I'd be happy to assist, sir," he said seriously.

Detective Chavez smiled. "No, I'm not serious, Jeff. It's my responsibility, but thanks anyway. I'll see you at the detention center."

CHAPTER
FORTY

It had been a long night. Detective Chavez had taken care of the necessary paperwork, hurried home, showered, changed into a fresh suit, and headed back to the office to wait for the appointed time for the search of the St. Claire home to take place. Meanwhile, he requested assistance from two fellow homicide detectives, Harrison Stidwell and Brad Martinez, who were currently between cases and more than happy to help the detective.

When Detective Chavez reached the St. Claire residence, he parked in the driveway. He walked over to the patrol car officer, who had been watching the residence through the night.

"Good Morning, Officer. I'm Detective Chavez, and I'll be doing the search this morning. I appreciate your watching over the residence all night. We'll take it from here."

"Great. Nothing at all to report, Detective. I'm off in thirty, so you timed it perfectly. Good luck to you." He started his car and drove off.

Detectives Stidwell and Martinez drove up, parked in front of the house, and once out of their car, walked up to Detective Chavez for instructions.

"Okay, fellows, both parties who live here are in custody, and the premises have been watched all night by one of our officers, so there's no need to worry about anyone being in the residence."

He led the way to the front door and reached inside his coat pocket for the key he had obtained from Helen.

"I know you know your job, but be very conscientious about the search. I don't want anything screwed up and thrown out in court because of our mistake. I want this bastard to get what he deserves for killing the old lady."

"Understandable," said Harrison.

"Brad, you start in the kitchen. Harrison, you take the bedrooms on the front side of the house. I'll start in the master bedroom at the back of the house." He handed each detective a copy of the search warrant. "The items we're looking for are listed, and I need you to be careful to complete the paperwork properly. I know you're familiar with the case, but if you have any questions, let me know. Don't overlook anything that we can use to fry this guy."

They entered the home, and each detective went to his designated area to begin the search. They donned gloves and started their search. The first item that came down the stairs was the silver laptop Harrison had found in an upstairs bedroom, which had apparently been used as an office. This item would be delivered to Cyber Crime Unit for intensive search efforts to find websites that had been used to obtain information regarding any criminal activity. Harrison set the computer by the front door and returned to the front bedrooms in search of other items on the search-warrant list.

Brad searched the kitchen and found nothing until he reached the tall double-door cabinet that held the everyday food-staple items. He opened the doors and carefully viewed every object on the top shelf and worked his way down the five shelves until he reached the bottom shelf. The shelf held boxes of aluminum foil, plastic wrap, boxes of large plastic bags, and paper items such as napkins, paper plates, paper bowls, and plastic utensils. He reviewed the items listed on the warrant and pulled from the cupboard the paper bowls that were still in the plastic bag, and the box of plastic spoons, and he grabbed the box of large plastic bags. He retrieved the paper evidence bag he had brought and placed the seized items in it. All items seized had to be checked against those recovered from the trash can and then stored as evidence from the crime. All items would then be compared for similarities, such as brand names, dates purchased and/or dates of expiration—anything that might identify that it was from the same source.

Detective Chavez was still searching the master bedroom. He was meticulous about searching every nook and cranny since it had been his experience that the bedroom, being the most intimate room in someone's home, was usually where items of value might be hidden.

Value was relative, he thought. Secrecy had a value all its own, since it related to many things, like sex acts of the individual, the couple, or many individuals, or secrecy related to a murder. You never could anticipate what would be found in a bedroom of someone's castle. In his fifteen years in the homicide unit, he'd found some pretty strange things.

He went from the main area to the master closet. He searched every inch, including the pockets in clothing, the lining of clothing, hats, and whatever else might be kept on the shelf above the clothes, and then he turned his attention to the floor. He checked every single shoe on the closet floor and found nothing. As the detective exited the closet, he noticed a corner of the carpet upturned. He knelt down and pulled the corner of carpeting up to find a man's black sock underneath. As he picked it up, he noticed it held something inside. He dumped the items out of the sock and into the palm of his gloved hand. There sat the two rings Helen had described and provided a picture of. "Gotcha, you SOB." He exited the closet and headed downstairs.

"Hey, fellows," he said loudly. "Looks like we got our man." He showed Brad the rings in his hand. Harrison came down the steps to see what the commotion was about.

"Good work, Chavez." Harrison pulled a plastic evidence bag from his pocket and assisted the detective with the rings.

"I'm done with the master bedroom. How are your fellows doing?"

"Done. Ready for the next area," said Harrison as he put the bagged rings in the paper evidence sack.

"Me too," responded Brad.

"Good. Harrison, you take the front room. Brad, you take the family room, and I'll head out into the garage."

Each departed to their assigned areas. Detective Chavez went out the door that led to the garage. He immediately saw what he was looking for. There on a shelf above a wooden workbench he spotted another can of the red-chili sauce that was a duplicate of the one found in the trash can by the homeless fellow. This can had the same thick black ink that stated RECALLED on the front of the can, and on the top of the workbench among several tools strewn about was a box of latex gloves, size medium. Brad came out to the garage.

"Nothing in the family room, Detective. What have you got there?"

"Medium gloves." He held the box up with his gloved hands for Brad to clearly see.

"The dumb shit used a glove size much too small for his hand, and that's why he left fingerprints and a palm print."

"Yeah, if it wasn't for stupid criminals and forensics, our job would be much harder." He laughed.

"I think that's everything on our list. I'll complete the search of the garage, and we'll get out of here."

"Okay, I'll let Harrison know." He went back into the house.

Fifteen minutes later, the three detectives were ready to exit the home. As they left with the seized items, Detective Chavez locked the door and placed a police seal at the edge of the door and its frame. He dated and initialed it. He would know if anyone entered the house in his absence. He carried out the same procedure at the back door in the garage.

"Thanks for your help, fellows."

"No problem," said Harrison as he entered the driver's side of the unmarked car. Brad waived as he entered the other side.

Detective Chavez was feeling pretty cocky with the evidence he'd obtained and was thrilled the evidence would most likely guarantee Bill's conviction. He'd drop it off at the evidence bureau, and then call to inform Judge Marks of the outcome of the warrants he had signed the night before.

CHAPTER
FORTY-ONE

Several weeks later, Detective Chavez entered the conference room on the third floor of the district attorney's office. The room had a wall of windows, which looked out over the city it served, and a long polished cherry wood table, which filled most of the room.

"Ah, Detective Chavez, come and meet Clifton Diaz and Ashley Long, attorneys-at-law. They represent Bill and Helen St. Claire."

The detective shook hands with the attorneys and then pulled the black leather chair away from the table and sat.

"Mr. Diaz, Ms. Long, if I do say so myself, it looks like we have an open and shut case against your clients," said the DA.

"We are aware of the evidence that was seized at their home. I think we need to discuss the possibility of a plea bargain in this matter," said Mr. Diaz, while Ms. Long nodded in assent.

The district attorney smiled at the detective. "What did you have in mind?"

Mr. Diaz spoke up before Ms. Long could. "No death penalty for Bill. He'll agree to life."

Ms. Long then added. "I was thinking five to ten years for Helen. After all, she did lead you down the path of discovery."

They waited quietly and patiently for the response from the district attorney. "I'll assume you've cleared this with your clients, right?"

"Yes of course," said Ashley Long.

Clifton simply nodded.

The detective sat and said nothing while the three negotiated the lives of Helen and Bill.

"Helen is a victim as much as anyone in this matter," Ashley Long argued. "All her life she's been submissive to Bill. I think five to ten is appropriate."

The district attorney looked at Detective Chavez. "Do you have any input, Detective?"

"Yes. I watched as Bill manipulated Helen while I interviewed him. I agree, she most likely was a victim of this as well as Mrs. Murphy." He paused. "The only piece of the puzzle I haven't solved, but will if need be, is the silver Subaru. Did Bill tell you about that?" He waited for the attorney's reply.

Mr. Diaz knew the question had been directed to him. "We'll give you whatever you need, even if only to satisfy your curiosity, but only if you agree to our terms." He looked at the district attorney, knowing it was his decision that would determine the final outcome.

The district attorney looked at Detective Chavez and then spoke. "Whatever the final decision is, I think both your clients are getting a deal they don't deserve. What with the evidence we have, the premeditation, and the horrific aspects of killing a harmless old lady that didn't have a chance to defend herself, your clients would easily get the maximum of any sentence allowed." He paused. "I'll agree to fifteen to twenty for Helen. After all, this was her mother that she conspired to kill, and I'll agree to life without the possibility of parole for Bill." He looked again at Detective Chavez. "Have any problem with that, Detective?"

"We'll take the deal." Mr. Diaz said quickly and got up to shake hands with the district attorney in an effort to seal the deal, and then with Detective Chavez.

"And?" Detective Chavez said, waiting for the response to his question.

"It was his cousin's silver Subaru. He borrowed it the night before the incident."

"It isn't an incident, Mr. Diaz. It was a cold-blooded murder," the detective said sternly.

"If that's all, I'll take my leave to type up the required paperwork. Good day, gentlemen." The attorney walked around the table to exit the conference room.

"Are you sure you won't reconsider for Helen? After all, she's in ill health, what with her bad back and all?" Ashley batted her eyes at the district attorney.

"Nope. It's a take-it-or-leave-it proposition, Ms. Long. Your client's ill health is what I would consider a personal problem. She willingly participated in the crime and now has to do the time."

Ashley hesitated before finally agreeing to fifteen to twenty, hoping Helen would get out on parole long before she reached either mark. "Okay. I'll get the paperwork prepared for the judge's signature. Thank you." She grabbed her briefcase and left the room without the cordial handshake to either gentleman.

"Job well done, Detective. Your quick and astute work has saved the taxpayers a bundle of money in trial costs." The district attorney patted his back as he turned to leave the conference room.

"Thanks." Detective Chavez was pleased with the outcome. His hard work had caused two cold-blooded killers to be put away, and that was satisfying. Tomorrow he'd go back to the office and resume reviewing cold cases until the next murder took place in his jurisdiction. He left the conference room with a sense of pride in the work he had done, and felt ready to take on the next case.